MW00987203

Down the
Road a Piece

Joseph G. Sissón

Cover Design by Donald J. Barrie
Edited by Laura Watson; Kathryn F. Galán, Wynnpix Productions

This is a work of fiction. Names, characters, places, brands, media, and incidents are either the product of the author's imagination or are used fictitiously. Any resemblance to similarly named places or to persons living or deceased is unintentional.

Hardcover print ISBN: 979-8-4024-0355-0
Paperback print ISBN: 979-8-5175-7452-7

To parents who struggle to give their children a better life
than they endured

CONTENTS

AUTHOR'S NOTE

The story depicted in *Down the Road a Piece* took place in 1957. I was thirteen, lived in a diverse community in San Diego, California, attended private Catholic schools, and, as a Boy Scout, attained the rank of Eagle Scout. My parents worked hard to give me a better life than they'd had but offered no guide to prepare me for what I learned during the family's summer sojourn on Route 66 through the Deep South to visit relatives in Missouri, Tennessee and Mississippi. My parents' childhood lore first came alive the day I helped them prepare the meals for our trip. My increased awareness throughout the journey compromised my innocence and brought me to my coming of age as a young man.

Interspersed with lighthearted family fun were grueling events that caused confusion and hurt. Like the protagonist, I blamed my misunderstandings on my father, but I returned home with new insights about my country and an appreciation for my father's struggles that showed me how entering manhood was more than just a trip down the road a piece.

Years after that vacation, my siblings and I continue to talk about our 1957 summer vacation experiences; reviewing Dad's tape recordings helps our recall. Of course, these actual conversations were not perfectly remembered, but I record them as closely as possible.

After writing this story, I discovered a publishing gate that was established during the Berlin Conferences of 1884-1885 for the European partitioning of the African continent. One agreement included standardizing literature-writing rules that held at bay all women's and especially nonwhite people's stories. Nowadays, self-publishing, like the printing press, offers a means for those writers including me to participate and share in a reality denied by the earlier gatekeepers.

Many contemporary English-language style and usage guides have adopted a rule, which I believe subliminally supports systemic racial divisions, to capitalize skin-color adjectives and racial group descriptions. Though readers likely will not take note of this element in my book, I elected to refuse to kowtow to that political scheme around historically created racial identities and have not capitalized the words *white*, *negro*, or *black*. The author of *The Warmth of Other Suns*, Isabel Wilkerson, didn't capitalize words related to people, either. Ta-Nehisi Coates referred to the enslaved as *the tasked*. So, I am not the first author to be sensitive to marginalizing those not of the power structure.

MISSISSIPPI

1.

I've seen so much since we left San Diego six short weeks ago. Too much. Right now, I want to forget everything that happened in Mississippi. I'm thirteen, and just after my birthday a few weeks ago, my family left on a vacation to meet relatives, including my parents' siblings, and their children.

Mississippi. Everything always comes back to *Mississippi.*

Though we started our trip in June, it's now a hot, late-July evening. We're leaving a restaurant near Oklahoma City, Oklahoma, on our return trip home to Southern California. As my family walks to the car, my mother stops in the middle of the parking lot.

"It beats the heck out of me why, ever since we left your Aunt Myra's, you've avoided your dad," she blurts out loud to me and then stands there, waiting for an answer.

I say nothing.

She shakes her head. "Go ahead, catch up with your brothers."

My brother James is fourteen months younger than I am, a few inches shorter, and, like me, has rusty brown skin and tight curly hair. He runs ahead and jerks open the back passenger door. "Shotgun!" he shouts and smirks at me.

"Gaylloyd," Mom calls before I have a chance to contest his claim to the window seat. "Please come here."

She and Dad stand by the driver's door.

"Dad has driven this whole trip," she says, her back to the car as she focuses on me. "You practiced driving before we left Aunt Myra's. Dad says you did well. You're the oldest, and we think you're grown up enough to help him drive. We'll get home faster with both of you taking turns."

My heart feels as if it will leap from my body. "You want me to drive?" Mom nods. "I'm going to help Dad drive?" My voice quakes. "Mom, thanks." Just for a minute, I forget the last few weeks.

"Daddy, is Gaylloyd driving?"

James's question pierces our siblings' sing-song, "Gaylloyd's going to dri-ive. Gaylloyd's going to dri-ive."

"This I've got to see," my skeptical seven-year-old brother, Phillip, murmurs. The other boys bounce and wrestle on the back seat, still singing the chant.

Dad stoops to look in the car. "Quiet down. Yes, Gaylloyd will help me drive." His deep voice stops the ruckus.

I want to hug him, but then I remember and hold back.

Mississippi

BEFORE LEAVING
2.

Early June in my hometown, San Diego, brings the first evening out of school for the summer. Seventh grade was tough, but eighth should be easier. I'll soon be a grown man, like my friends. At my bedside, I kneel to recite my nightly prayers beneath a small color print of three angels who have shoulder-length, blond hair and enormous, white, feathered wings.

Two of my brothers, James and Michael, are on their knees at the bottom of their bunk bed. They compete in harmony with me. "Amen." We three older brothers sleep in one bedroom and the three younger ones in another.

Mom and Dad stand in the doorway, smiling and nodding. His tall, lean frame towering over her, although she's not small in stature. Her black hair falls below her waist in loose ringlets, though normally she wears it rolled into a tight bun at the nape of her neck. Her stomach bulges slightly under her robe. He puts his arm around her shoulders.

"Sleep tight, boys," she whispers.

James clambers up a ladder to the top bunk. Standing on a high rung, he says, "Don't let the bed bugs bite." It's something he repeats every night. I'm sure he relishes the alliteration. I don't know anything about bed bugs, and I shrug. He giggles as he rolls under his covers.

Michael laughs and crawls into the bottom bed. The bunk is against a wall opposite the window where I sleep. His hair curls in loopy springs like Mom's, and his skin is as dark as Dad's.

"Tomorrow, you'll help us get ready for our trip," Dad announces like a news bulletin.

James shouts, "We're going! Are we really going?" He looks down at Michael then across at me and then repeats, "We're really going!"

"Mommy, I can't sleep," I complain. "All I can think about is the cotton Dad told us about. I want to see what it looks like before they flatten it into underwear." I can't believe we have to wait two more days to leave.

Dad chuckles. "You'll sleep sound after I turn the lights off." I hear a click. The room is dark with only a waxing half-moon to brighten the windowsill.

I listen to Dad hum, "Swing Low, Sweet Chariot," as he follows Mom down the hall to the other kids' bedroom. The tune fades out.

Dad's right. My warm, comfortable bed and soft pillow are the last things I remember before my dreams are interrupted by the morning sun heating our Southern California town. "Up and at 'em," he calls. "Don't sleep your lives away."

Dad's wake-up call comes early on my first summer morning. School is out, but we never sleep past seven when his ship is in. He's been in the Navy since even before he married Mom. After a twenty-seven-year career, he just retired a few days ago. Having him at home all the time will certainly be different. He's promised to take us swimming, fishing, and hiking with the Boy Scouts.

After washing up, I go into the kitchen to help Mom.

"Gaylloyd, let me look at your face." She runs her thumb over my upper lip. "You need to wash this." She turns and adjusts my head for a better look.

"I did, Mom."

"Go into the bathroom, and wash your upper lip."

I can't imagine what she sees or how my lip got dirty. I just got up and haven't been outside. My reflection is the same, nothing different, but I wash anyway, especially scrubbing the area under my nose.

I come back ready to set the table.

"You didn't wash," Mom says and takes me back to the bathroom, where we stand in front of the sink. I still see nothing. She scrubs my upper lip, looks at it again, and works on it until I whimper.

"Oh my, it's peach fuzz. My boy's growing a mustache. He's becoming a man."

"Mom, it's been that way for a while."

"I never noticed," she murmurs.

I set the breakfast table, while Mom heaps steaming buckwheat pancakes on a platter. With a lot of chatter, my younger siblings scramble to their regular seats. James puts the maple syrup near the butter in the center, while Michael sets out drinking glasses and finds a place for the pitcher of cold milk that glistens with condensation. Dad places a bib on baby Mark in his highchair and blesses the meal.

Sliding into her seat, Mom reminds us, "Don't let your eyes be bigger than your stomachs. Help yourself only to what you can eat. There's plenty here. Clean your plates. You can always come back for more."

Phillip, so proud of himself, announces, "We belong to the clean plate club."

The last time Dad came home was from a tour in China. He gave us each a number instead of calling us by our names. I'm his Number One Son. He tells us, "That's what Chinese people do." Phillip, born on Oahu, is his Number Four Son. I often tease Number Four about his Hawaiian roots, because that's the state where we lived for four years.

I like bananas sliced on top of my pancakes, so I nod my head toward a wooden bowl full of fruit. "Hula Boy, pass a banana." I wait for him to react.

He drenches his pancakes with maple syrup. Calm, he looks up. "Oh, are you talking to me?"

"Yes, Grass Skirts, I am."

"Here." He hands a banana to Michael. "Pass this to the

number-one monkey."

Michael hands it to James. "Pass this."

"A gift from Hawaii," James jeers as he gives it to me.

"Number One," Dad says with an evil eye to each of us, me most of all. "We have a lot to do today. I don't want you squabbling with your brothers."

I lower my head and stare at my breakfast. Not that I'm sorry for egging Phillip on but for having Dad notice.

"Feed the baby," Mom says and hands me a tiny fork with a small bite of pancake for Mark, who just turned a year old.

Everyone eats and jabbers at once, including Mom and Dad, as they plan the day. I don't listen intently, but Dad's mention of chickens wiggles through all the other talk.

Mom wipes the baby's chin. "George, when the water gets hot, I'll bring it to the garage."

"Emma, you shouldn't carry anything heavy. I'll send the boys when we're ready. Gaylloyd and James will help dress the chickens."

I don't think to ask what they're talking about or what it means to "dress chickens." Dad looks at me. "After breakfast, you, James, and Michael catch the chickens and bring them to the garage. I'll be there waiting for you."

Like ducklings in a parade, James, Michael, Phillip, and even Charles, the second to the youngest, follow me out the kitchen door.

Mom stands on the porch and watches Charles trail the rest of us. She says, "He doesn't want to be left out."

Last year, at our annual church fair, I won five chickens in a coin toss game. They are the first animals I've ever had, other than our dog. The small, yellow, downy puffs with tiny orange feet peeped all day long. Now, as I stare at the four plump, dark-brown hens and the speckled black one, I wonder what Dad will do with them.

The chickens make a ruckus as we approach their coop.

Four-year-old Charles giggles, "You're going to catch a chicken?" he asks me as he grips one of Phillip's left fingers.

"I don't want to touch those chickens." Michael pulls his hands behind his back. "They might bite me."

Phillip says, "Chickens don't bite." He crosses his eyes at Michael. "They peck."

Because the cage is small, I know the birds can't get away, but I'm not sure how to catch them. I don't want to handle them any more than Michael does, but, because I'm the oldest, I must think of something.

"James," I study the pen. "Take off your shirt."

"Huh? Why? I'm not taking my shirt off. What are you going to do with it?"

"You know when we take a shower how you always whip your towel? Well, if you snap your shirt at the chickens, they'll move over to the far corner." I point. "They'll be easier to catch there. All you need to do is scare 'em. Don't hit 'em."

"Oh sure," he says and pulls his T-shirt over his head then winds it up. The *snap-snap* does the trick. The birds cower in the back corner of the cage.

The rest of us scream and wave our arms. "Shoo! *Shoo*!" The noise helps. I straddle the wire door and grab a wing, as it batts my arms, then I clutch the feet and hand the first upside-down bird to James.

I succeed in wrestling the second one and thrust it at Michael.

"I don't want to touch it," Michael complains. Sweat glues his curls to his forehead.

"Take it," I order.

He jerks his arm out but then pulls it back.

"Take it and hold tight!"

He squints and grabs the legs. The chicken writhes, squawks, and tries to get away, but Michael hangs on.

Phillip clasps the feet of the next one, looks up at me, and says nothing, but follows the first two.

Imitating him, Charles holds his prize with both hands and follows Phillip down the path to the garage. I grab the last one and hurry behind them.

When everything goes the way Dad wants, he smiles a lot.

"Great job," he says as I enter the attached garage with its overhead storage loft.

I hand my chicken to Dad and watch him tie its feet and lay it on the concrete floor with the others. Their chest feathers are flared, and their perked heads watch us, their captors. "Your Great-Aunt Myra and I worked together back on our farm in Winona," he says. "My job was to catch them, just like you did here this morning. Then she'd wring their necks."

I've never witnessed a neck wringing and have no idea what he's talking about. I'd lost count of the times Mom threatened to wring our necks. As mischievous as James is, his neck has been threatened the most. I've never seen anyone with a wrung neck. It doesn't sound good.

Phillip's already in the loft when I climb a ladder to find a spot near the edge to sit and watch. I swing my legs in a slow kicking motion. James and the rest stand behind Dad against the wall, near the back door.

"Phillip, do you want to sit next to me?"

Before he answers, he studies me. "No, I can see fine from here." He leans against the rustic wall, trying to be cool. I'm sure he doesn't know what to expect any more than I do.

Dad always tries to make sure we understand the ins and outs of things. He normally offers long, involved explanations. But not this time. He's serious. He picks the biggest chicken, removes the binding from its feet, and wraps his fingers around its head, its red comb sticking between them. Like a softball pitcher winding up for a pitch, he swings his arm. I hear a loud snap. A headless body soars into the air, wings swatting and feet kicking the emptiness. Frozen in horror, I watch the blood squirt from its neck with every heartbeat.

I'm fixated on the mass of brown feathers, watching it change directions several times. Then, in slow motion, all I see is the headless bloody bird fly helplessly, and land on me.

FRIED CHICKEN

3.

I don't hear myself scream or even remember my leap from the loft. "Mom! *Mom*!" I fling open the kitchen door.

She's seated next to the diapering table, changing Mark. "What, Gaylloyd?"

"I… I…" I rush to her, burying my head in her lap. My lips tremble and tears gush down my cheeks. She runs her hand over my close-cropped head as she cradles my face until my sobs subside.

"Attaboy," she says, dabbing my tears with her apron. "You'll be alright. Big boys don't cry, now do they?" She doesn't say anything about my bloody clothes, but her admonishment embarrasses me. I'm too old to act like a scaredy-cat.

I sniff, lift the pan lid, and look at the water heating on the stove. It hasn't come to a boil. On the **diaper table**, Mark peddles his feet in the air and squirms. I consider going back to the garage.

Mom finishes diapering the baby and lifts him. "You can help me until Daddy calls you. Wipe off the table and sweep the floor." She carries Mark from the room.

I put the broom away just as James comes in.

"Daddy wants you to bring the hot water," he says. "Pour it in the wash pan I put on the ground outside."

"I'll get it." As I reach for the heavy pot, steam spurts from under its clattering lid.

James smirks and reaches for the bouncing cover. "I'll get that for you."

"I don't need any help." I cast my eyes away from him. Firstborns don't run from headless chickens.

The steam stings my hands and eyes as I empty the kettle. My other brothers horse around with one another as Dad carries three headless chickens by their feet in one hand and two in the other. Gooey blood drips from their necks.

"You looked so funny running away from that chicken," Charles teases.

"All of 'em ran around, even the first one." Phillip grins. "I stayed out of the way."

Not looking at them, I ignore their comments.

Dad stands behind me. I'm grateful he says nothing about me running off. He lays the birds next to the galvanized wash pan on the lawn in front of the kitchen door. I never named those puffballs. With their life drained away, they seem smaller.

Michael leans near the fence with Charles and Phillip crowded around him. Dad dangles a chicken in front of James and me. "Dunk it like this." He swishes it back and forth in the water. "Be careful. The water's hot." He lays the soaking wet bird on the ground and gently pulls a fistful of feathers from its breast. The warm, wet down smells like damp moss in a forest. As we pluck, it seems even more musty and moldy than moss and gets pasted on everyone, even the three watching.

After we pluck all five chickens, James parades back and forth in front of the naked birds, hands on his hips, elbows flapping, and head bobbing to and fro. Charles chortles and runs to him. "Put some feathers on me!"

Dad grins. "Gaylloyd and James," he says, pointing to one of the orange trees near our vegetable garden, "empty the pan back there and meet us inside."

My left arm waves the air as my right hand grips the pot handle. I walk slowly to keep my balance, the water sloshing all the way. "Hurry," I say to James, who is struggling as much as I am. "I don't want to miss anything." After we dump the water, I lead the way into the house.

Mom looks up as we come in. "Wash up and help Daddy."

Dad stands near the kitchen sink, a white chef's apron around his waist. One chicken rests on the cutting board in front of him, James, and me; the rest are in the sink. With James standing on his left and me on his right, Dad hands knives to each of us. "Take the chicken I put in front of you, and cut from the hind end to the front," he says, demonstrating.

Not much different than cleaning fish. Stick the knife in its booty, slice past the stomach, and pull it open. I watch the innards ooze out. Dad sticks his hand inside and pulls. More intestines dangle through his fingers over a bowl in the sink. I feel nauseous, but I don't want to show it. I grasp the countertop to steady myself.

Dad laughs. "Your faces are twisted like I'm spilling *your* guts." Lifting each organ from the bowl, he shows us the gizzard, the liver, and the heart. "I'll chop these for the gravy."

Feeling better, I ask, "What's your favorite piece?"

He smacks his lips. "Son, well…" He thinks for a second. "It'll have to be the breast." He looks around and says real fast, "And all the rest" he laughs, squints his eyes, and shakes his head.

After we cut the chickens and rinse each piece, he puts several in a brown paper bag with just the right mixture of flour and spices. He shakes the bag to coat them and places the pieces in a sieve. Then he eases the batch into scalding oil, which makes crackling sounds. The spicy smells fill the kitchen air.

Mom leaves to answer the doorbell. "Come on in. I'm happy you could come."

"Hello, Cooke and Lullaby," Dad says to our next-door neighbors. Unlike Dad's, Mr. Cooke's tightly curled hair is on its way to gray. He works as a porter for the Santa Fe Railroad. Mrs. Cooke is lighter in complexion. "Michael, move over. Give Mr. and Mrs. Cooke room to sit."

Mom nods toward the avocado-colored banquette bench that encircles the kitchen table on three sides. Michael and Phillip stand on the bench cushion next to the stove, watching the chicken sizzle.

Mr. Cooke sits next to his wife after she scoots in. "George, let's talk about what you need us to do with the house while you're gone."

The sounds of frying chicken blend with lively banter and laughter as Dad tells Mississippi farm stories and washes a few more pieces of raw chicken in the sink. The kitchen buzzes with chatter over the sizzling crackles of the soon-to-be mouthwatering chicken.

"Daddy, is that oil hot?" Michael asks.

Dad turns his head to look. "Stick your hand in there, and see for yourself."

Laughing at dad's stupid suggestion, I sit next to Mrs. Cooke. Michael is quiet, staring at the bubbling oil. Phillip leans in for a better look.

Michael grabs his hand and dunks it.

"*Michael!*" I shout.

NEW CAR

4.

Phillip's piercing screams fill every nook of the kitchen. He holds his blistering hand to his chest and falls to the floor, rolling and wailing. Frozen in place, I cover my mouth.

Dad spins around, his face flushed. He yanks Michael off the bench and dangles him by his ankles above the deep fryer. "Boy, I ought to stick your head in there!"

"Daddy!" Michael hollers. "Daddy, *no!*"

Stunned, I watch Michael squirm upside down. I'm not the only one unable to intervene. No one tries to stop Dad. He lifts Michael away from the stove, sets him on the floor, and looks at Mr. and Mrs. Cooke, who stare at him.

He puts Phillip on his lap as Mom rushes from the kitchen and hurries back with cocoa butter and a towel. "My God! Look at his hand. Gaylloyd, put some water in a bowl!"

I fill a mixing bowl and hand it to her. When she **submerges Phillip's hand, he screams.**

"I should have watched more closely," Dad says under his breath. "I thought the boy knew I was jokin'."

Mom carefully rubs cocoa butter on Phillip's hand The motion detaches his dark skin **to reveal the bright-pinkish flesh underneath.**

Michael leans against the edge of the table and sobs as loud as Phillip. "I'm sorry."

After Dad and Phillip leave for the hospital and the neighbors go home, I put the chicken in the refrigerator. James wipes off the table, Charles plays with his trucks, and the baby sleeps. Mom takes Michael into our bedroom and closes the door. I hear her muffled voice above his weeping, but I can't make out what she says.

I hope the doctors can heal Phillip's hand. There's a boy in my school who burnt his right hand when he was small. His fingers curl like an eagle's claw, preventing him from using it except to hit the tether ball. I wonder if that will happen to my brother.

Four hours later, Dad returns with Phillip. "This is a fine howdy-do," he says to Mom. "I don't want this accident to ruin our trip. We'll just have to take extra-good care of Phillip. The nurse gave me enough medical supplies to last a lifetime and a list of military hospitals along the way, if we need one."

He turns to James, Michael, and me sitting at the kitchen table. "I need you boys to help us get ready for our trip." He looms over us, "Now, stay out of trouble."

That night in bed, I listen as he plays our grand piano in the living room. Oscar Hammerstein's "Ol' Man River" wafts into every room in the house. Probably even the neighbors hear him singing; it wouldn't be the first time.

I try to imagine how Phillip's hand looks under the layered gauze. My heavy eyelids close as the music changes to Dad's favorite boogie-woogie tune, "Down the Road a Piece."

* * *

The next day, I find Mom in my three youngest brothers' room, choosing what they'll need for the trip. There are two suitcases lined up against the wall under the window. She looks up from sorting their socks. "Gaylloyd, I want you to choose a suitcase and pack. You'll need church clothes and two pairs of everyday pants and shirts. Don't forget your underwear."

"Yes, Mom." I smile as I study which suitcase I want. Taking the biggest one to my room, I open it on my bed and start to pack.

James comes in and peers over my shoulder. "What're you doing?"

"What does it look like? I'm packing my clothes and a couple books." I slide *Alice in Wonderland* off a shelf and leaf through to see how many pages it has. It's actually two books in one, including *Through the Looking Glass*, another Lewis Carroll story. I put it on top of my shirts.

James grabs the book. "Don't put it in there." He throws it on my bed. "There's no room for my things. Mom told me I have to put my stuff in with yours." He goes to the dresser and pulls out shirts, pants, and underwear then dumps his clothes in a crumbled-up pile on top of mine. "There," he says and smiles.

I shake my head. "You can't do that."

"Do what?"

"Throw them in like that." I toss his things back at him. "Fold them first."

"Who made you the king of packing?"

"They won't fit if they're not folded."

"Oh yeah?" He storms out, slamming the door.

"Come back here." I open the door, chase after him, grab his shirt, and pull him backward.

Dad stands in front of us, arms crossed over his chest. James jerks away from me.

"I told you boys I don't want trouble. I'll be back in ten minutes with a switch, and if your things aren't packed…" He pokes his index finger into James's chest. "I'm gonna wear out your behind."

I turn, leaving Dad with James, and go into my younger brothers' room. Mom has two open cases on their bed beside piles of clothes to be packed. I ask her, "Do you want help?"

"Here, put these in that big bag on the pillow." She hands me two shirtwaist dresses and a full pleated skirt, all of them folded, and a hat box.

"What's in here?" Inside the box, I find a hat that looks like a halo with feathers. "Mom, it's beautiful."

"Thank you. I made it for a contest at church and won first prize. I found the right color ribbon and attached those quail feathers. That one's for me. I'm taking another one I made for Aunt Myra."

Dad saunters in, his broad smile stretching from one side of his face to the other. "Honey, we're going for a ride."

"Where are we going?"

"We're buying a car."

Mom looks up from packing. "What's wrong with the one we have?"

"It's bad enough we have to worry about Phillip's hand. I don't want to worry about breakdowns while we're on the road. It might be hard for us to find a place to get the car fixed."

She studies him. "Oh, for Pete's sake." She shakes her head. "Why didn't you think of this a week ago?"

* * *

At the car lot, Dad's hard bargaining seems more with Mom than with the salesman. Her back is to him as she holds the baby. James is at her side. "Let's just get something reasonable," she says.

Dad circles a dark-green 1957 Packard and then sits behind the steering wheel. "Look at this," he says to Mom. "The window sticker shows it even has electric windshield wipers." He reaches over, opens the front passenger door, and pats the seat. "Honey, sit here. Just see what this one feels like."

I decide to check out the other cars while they make up their minds. I wander into the showroom and over to a brand-new Chevy, blue with a white top and fantail trim. I climb into the passenger side.

A blonde girl, maybe a year or two younger than me, sits in the driver's seat, pretending she's driving. "Let's race that yellow car." She points out the window to a Ford convertible outside, on the far side of the car lot. "That's my mom and dad looking at it. She likes that car. I think my dad is going to buy it for her."

"Can I drive this one?"

"Yeah." She gets out, and I scoot over. After she's seated, she tells me, "You've got to rev it up first."

We roar as loud as we can, playing that we're racing away. Michael and Phillip crawl into the back.

Bouncing, Phillip holds the back of my seat with his bandaged hand. "What're you doing?" he asks.

"We're racing that yellow car over there."

"We'll help you," Michael says.

"Okay." I make the sounds of the engine starting, and everyone chimes in. "We're in first." I pretend to shift to second, and we get louder. Then I put the car in third. We yell at the top of our lungs.

"Hey, what're you kids doing?" a salesman hollers from the front office. He hurries toward us, his green tie flipping over his shoulder as he comes to the car, glaring at me. He sticks his head through the window on my side. "Missy, your parents would have a fit if they saw you playing with these…" He stares to the back, where my brothers are seated. "*Boys*." He pulls his head back out of the car. "You boys get over there to your parents."

All of us climb out.

"You can stay," the man says to the girl. He moves between her and Michael and puts his hand on her shoulder. "I don't think your folks would mind you being here." He turns to face me and my brother, easing her behind him.

"Our parents don't care that we're over here either," I say.

The man swivels around and glares at me. "Maybe not, but I want them to keep an eye on all of you."

I push Michael's shoulder. "Come on, guys."

My brothers follow me outside, where Dad and Mom are talking to a salesman in a blue seersucker suit and red tie. He's pitching the car. "You might not know this, but automatics are the pride of the automobile industry these days." He stands next to the vehicle, biting his bottom lip. "Ma'am, this car will comfortably seat your whole family." He steps away from the Packard as his eyes dart from Dad to the showroom and back. "We also have nice used cars on the lot across the street. Why don't we walk over there? Perhaps you'll find one more in your price range."

My parents look at him but say nothing, their faces blank as if he isn't there.

"This car has a radio," he adds, smiling. "And there's plenty of room in the trunk." He walks to the back and opens it. "Of course, as I said before, we also have less expensive cars." He points to the used car lot again.

"No, but thank you," Dad says. "The sticker price says two thousand, one hundred. Will cash give me a better price?"

The salesman stands taller. "How much are we talking about?"

"Let's knock it down by three hundred."

"We might have a deal, but I have to talk to my manager." He practically sprints back to the showroom.

I walk to Dad and kick the front tire on the driver's side.

"What're you doing?"

"I saw a man do that on a TV commercial."

"What do you expect to find out?"

"I don't know," I admit.

The salesman comes back with someone else who looks important, dressed in a black suit and tie. "Sir," he says, "I'm Rodney Young, owner and manager of this establishment. It would be a pleasure to negotiate a price we both can live with, but our cars are already at rock bottom. Three hundred dollars is a significant discount. Maybe too much. Is this beyond your budget?"

"I've checked prices with other car dealers," Dad says. "I like what you have, and I'm ready to drive this car off the lot for a thousand, nine hundred. I'll even throw in my car." He points to where it's parked near the showroom. "It's that black '52 Ford. Is that fair enough?"

"Five years? It's a pretty old car. Let's take a look."

Dad leads Mr. Young to our car. "It's in fine shape. I drive it only when my ship's in port." As we circle it, Dad opens the hood.

Mr. Young whistles. "I'm surprised to see how clean you've kept the engine."

Dad stands straighter, even more than usual. "I take good care of it."

Mr. Young kicks a tire. Dad looks at me and rolls his eyes. I grin.

"You drive a hard bargain, but I guess we can make it work. If you and your wife will come to my office, I'll write up the contract."

Dad holds out his hand. Mr. Young looks at it, then the car, before shaking his hand. They begin heading for the office.

I grab Dad's arm. "What about us?"

"Wait in the showroom," he says and leads the away.

"But that other guy said to stay with you." I point to the man.

Mr. Young frowns. "You boys can sit on that bench and wait for your parents. Don't wander around."

The girl is standing in front of her parents, across the showroom, her dad's right hand on her shoulder and his arm around her mother. She waves at me. They look happy. I wave back.

ON THE ROAD

5.

The ordeal at the car lot is finally over, thank goodness. Mom and Dad took forever, though, and the wooden bench in front of Mr. Young's office grew mighty hard to sit on. I couldn't imagine what they had to talk about while I kept my brothers from sneaking off. Now, they're mad at me.

Dad says, "We're celebrating." We pile into our new car and drive to a fancy Italian restaurant owned by his college friend. I order more spaghetti and meatballs than I can eat.

When Dad asks for the bill, his friend refuses to let him pay anything. "To your health and that of your family. We wish you a safe journey."

* * *

Early Friday morning, and without any fanfare, Dad eases our new car down the driveway. His erect posture makes me feel proud. I sit tall in the front seat between him and my mom and push my shoulders back into the seat.

"This is the trip of a lifetime," he exclaims.

Mom nods and smiles.

From the backseat, Phillip taps Dad's shoulder. "Has Aunt

Myra seen you in your Navy uniform?"

"That reminds me. Emma, did you bring pictures of our house?"

"Dad, didn't you tell us about Aunt Myra's big white house with a front porch?" I ask.

Charles pulls on the back of Mom's seat. "Is Mississippi farther than Los Angeles?"

Cranking my head around, I tell him, "It's farther than Hawaii and in the opposite direction." When I was a kid, before I was even in school, we sailed on a ship to Hawaii. We returned to San Diego by seaplane, my first time on a plane. Phillip was four. The trees and houses and everything familiar slowly disappears beneath us.

"I remember our first day at St. Jude's Academy," James says. I kneel on my seat to face my brothers in the back.

"The nuns wouldn't let me go to the third grade when we got to San Diego," I tell him, "because the schools in Hawaii were no good." I pause to see if Mom has anything to say about it.

"I thought it was because you couldn't spell." James grins like a Cheshire cat.

"When I lived in Hawaii," Phillip says, "the rain was so warm, I just stayed outside and played on the beach."

"Number Four, what else do you remember about Hawaii?" Dad asks.

"How can you remember anything about Hawaii? You were so small when we left. Whatever you know is because we told you."

"Oh yeah?" he blurts. "When I was little, I remember running away from waves."

"You're still a little pipsqueak."

His eyes water. "No, I'm not. I'm nine years old."

"No one as young as you were can remember anything about Hawaii," I say.

"How do you know what I remember?"

"See the orange trees," Dad says.

Mom smiles at him.

We take forever to reach Cleveland National Forest in the mountains, where we descend into the desert. The three youngest,

Phillip, Charles, and Mark, fall asleep before we get there. There's an abundance of scroungy sagebrush and small scrub trees amidst the scorched sand and rocks, but the cacti are sparse. Khaki-colored cliffs and giant boulders tower above the road on one side casting strange long shadows. A white waterfall cascades from sharp precipices into a stream that twists and flows around outcroppings then slithers through the arid land, stalking a town called Ocotillo in the near distance. We pass its one gas station, three stores, and a small, circular, sandy, treeless park between the stores.

Michael stares longingly out the car window at shallow, sky-blue creeks. "I wish we could stop and play in the water."

Dad looks over at it. "We need to get to St. Louis as soon as we can. What I'm looking for is a rest stop for lunch."

The perspiration makes Mom's hair curl against her neck. She lifts it and dries her shoulders with her handkerchief. "Oh my, it's hot!" After dampening the cloth with water, she leans across my lap to wipe Dad's forehead.

His eyes crinkle as he touches her hand.

Mom turns to my younger brothers in the back. "It's so hot in here. Roll down the windows. We need some fresh air."

"Here's where we'll stop for lunch." Dad turns into an open area and stops near a picnic table under a flowering acacia tree. Bees visit, flying from its branches to others nearby in the park. "We will stretch our legs and eat here, but we're not staying long."

The break is just what we need to run off energy. We scamper from the car to explore the park while Dad and Mom put our picnic lunches on the table. James helicopters in a complete circle, his arms outstretched at the prickly saguaros around us. "Look at all the cactuses."

Last year, James and I earned one of our Boy Scout merit badges for studying cactuses. "When you're in the desert, you can get water from a barrel cactus," he explains to Michael, who's not old enough to be in the Scouts.

As Dad and Mom set the table, James scoops up a carving knife. "Be careful with that," Mom warns.

"Don't worry. We're going to cut a barrel cactus and see if it really has water. Come on!" James yells. "Let's look for one." He dashes toward a group of the pale-green plants and chooses one about ten inches wide and as high as my knee. Three yellow flowers bloom on top, while long needles grow along its vertical ridges.

As Michael and I run up, James grasps the top, about to cut it open. "*Ouch*!" He snatches his hand to his chest. "These thorns are sharp." He smears blood on my arm, and I jump back, swinging at him open-handed but miss. With a handful of sand, I scrub off the blood.

"Look at this," he says, poking the spongy flesh inside.

I say, "Cut a piece, and squeeze the water into your hand."

He dribbles the juice into his cupped palm. "It's yellow."

"Taste it," I dare him.

He sips it, spits it out and throws the rest of the juice on the ground. "Yuck. It's nasty. Who drinks this stuff? I thought it would taste like water from the faucet."

"Birds and other animals like it. It's their only source of liquid here in the desert."

Mom calls us. "Boys, come and get it!"

James drops the cactus and races us back.

* * *

After I finish lunch, I gallop down a nearby gully of dry tumbleweeds, riding a make-believe horse and hollering like a cowboy. James tears after me, holding a drumstick in one hand and pumping it over his head like a war club. Michael leaves most of his lunch on his paper plate and follows. I guess he doesn't want to be left behind.

I find a route down into a wash, where a horned toad scurries into the sand. Several leggy jackrabbits scatter across our path, daring us to chase them.

I yell, "*Stop*!" and freeze. Michael is behind me and pushes me into James, who has taken the lead. "Quiet!"

A rattle interrupts the silence.

Michael hollers, "It's a snake!" and grabs the back of my shirt.

"I see it." I point to a nearby outcrop of rocks almost hidden by dry sagebrush. "It's a diamondback." A gray-white snake with dark, diamond-like markings is coiled near the shade of an immense boulder. "See it?"

The rattler warns us again, lifting its head to stare at us. I back up, holding onto James in front and Michael behind me, careful not to stumble. The snake eases its rattling to a stop and takes its time to slither under a big stone.

"Wow." Michael gasps. "That was a close call."

I turn and dash back to the table, where Mom and Dad are packing leftovers. "We saw a rattlesnake!" I shout, getting everyone's attention, especially Mom's.

"A rattlesnake? Where?" Then points at each of us as we run up, counting. "Get in the car, boys. It's time to go, now! George, did you hear what the boys said? They saw a rattlesnake."

"Yes, dear. They saw a rattler." He smiles. "Snakes do live out here!"

I guzzle water from a bottle while Dad packs the chest into the trunk. "Gaylloyd, put that cup in the box. Make sure we have everything. Look under the tables." He checks again, slams the trunk closed, and climbs in. "We need to get along, little doggies."

"Did you hear that?" James laughs as he opens the front door. "Daddy said *get along little doggies*, like the song. Good one, Daddy." Then he tries to scoot in ahead of me. "Gaylloyd, I get to sit next to Daddy. You've been sitting next to him all the way. It's my turn."

"That's because I'm the oldest." I lean in over him.

"Doesn't matter."

"Take turns." Mom finishes filling the trunk and covers everything with the table cloth. "James, you get in the front between Dad and me."

I feel I'm being treated like the younger kids but silently get in the seat behind Mom next to a window. Dad eases out of the parking lot and checks both ways, though there are no other cars on the road.

Being out of the hot sun is a relief, even though the car is not much cooler. With the windows down, warm air rushes over my sweaty cheeks.

"What kind of bird is that?" Charles points to one undulating in flight alongside the car, flashing its golden underwings before landing on a tall cactus.

Phillip says, "It's a tawny woodpecker."

"Know-it-all," James teases.

Ignoring him, Phillip adds, "The saguaro cactus reminds me of people stretching out their arms."

Charles giggles, crooks his arms at odd angles, and tumbles sideways onto my lap.

"It's sure dry around here." James turns around, kneeling on the front seat to look at us in the back.

"I wonder when it rained last," I say.

Phillip continues, oblivious to what James said. "The saguaros benefit wildlife by providing nectar and fruit for birds, bats, and insects."

"Stick your arms out, you guys," Michael insists.

We stretch our arms in various contortions, trying to outdo one another.

"Mommy, Michael hit me," Charles accuses.

"You boys settle down," she tells us. "Play a quiet game."

I invent a game called "talking cactus." We all interrupt our brothers, making up a story about what we think the cactus people are saying. We laugh as each new part of the story becomes more outrageous than the last.

"The Missus went shopping and the Mister stayed home to cut the grass!" Charles says.

"What grass?" We burst out giggling.

Mom wrinkles her face like a prune. "I wish you'd all be quiet."

"Mommy," James asks, tipping his head sideways toward her, "may I pleeease tell one more?"

She whispers, "Do it in your quiet voice. Do you think you can do that?"

Under his breath, James says, "My story is about a cactus cowboy crawling across the desert, looking for water. He slices

open a barrel cactus and drinks so much, he gets a tummy ache."
His voice gets louder as he describes the vomit the man spits up. I
don't know why any of us think this is funny, but our peals of
delight interrupt his story.

We quiet down when Phillip puts his finger to his lips and says,
"*Shhh*!"

Soon, we're restless again and play hand-slap.

Dad says above the hubbub, "How about playing the license
plate game?"

We like the idea and spot plates from California, Nevada,
Arizona, and New Mexico, even two from British Columbia,
Canada. We wave to other kids as we pass and speculate about the
ones who don't wave back.

Phillip sees a family and says, "Now take those guys. Their
great-grandma lives in San Bernardino. They're on their way to a
cemetery to dig a grave for their cat."

"Those people from Pennsylvania," says James. "I bet they're
going to Los Angeles to buy a poodle."

"A pink poodle," says Michael.

"You know, on television," I add, "the newscaster said
Hollywood movie stars are dyeing their poodles different colors."

We all burst out laughing and propose a rainbow of colors
poodles could be.

"I want a purple dog," Charles says.

"I think we should keep its natural color," says Michael.

"Boys, what would you like to sing?" asks Mom. "I'm tired of
your dog stories."

"You start off, Mom," says James.

She sings, "'Row, row, row your boat...'"

We all join her. I nudge James.

He nods at Mom. "She's singing."

Phillip smiles.

At home, we often gather around the piano to sing with Dad,
but Mom seldom joins in. Sometimes, when I'm in the kitchen doing
my homework while she's getting dinner ready, I hear her softly
sing a Billie Holiday song to herself.

Dad grins at her. "Mom, you're such a good sport." She smiles back at him. He starts a different song. We harmonize, changing words and creating verses that describe what we see along the road. It keeps our spirits high.

As darkness falls, the air begins to cool.

"Help Mark climb on the back window ledge, so he can take a nap," Mom says to me. Michael and I help him up, and he goes right to sleep. There's plenty of room for him to lie there, even to turn over when he needs to.

At our next gas stop, it's dark. Mom changes Phillip's bandage. I muscle between my brothers to see his hand. She gently takes his hand, but before she begins to unwrap the bandage, he whimpers. "Mommy, it hurts."

"Sweetheart, I'll be careful. Let me look at it." She lays his wrapped hand on her lap.

He squirms and pulls back. I laugh. She hasn't even cut the gauze yet. She struggles with him but finally unwraps it. His hand isn't as swollen, and the gauze is easier to remove. The open wound still makes me queasy, but it looks better.

* * *

I thought the car was huge when Dad bought it, but with all eight of us in it, getting comfortable is a challenge. Mom reads to us, and we try to sleep. Dad drives just under the speed limit and stops for fifteen minutes to catnap now and then.

When I'm up front again, I ask, "Are you all right, Dad?"

"Yes, son. Are you looking forward to meeting Aunt Myra?"

"I sure am."

"Great. That's what keeps me going."

BETWEEN HERE AND THERE

6.

I'm sure Dad said it was after midnight, but that was about two hours ago. The car bounces along, unsuccessfully dodging potholes, until it's on the paved parking lot of a circular diner.

Dad says, "Welcome to Albuquerque, New Mexico, boys. Get out of the car and use the restroom while we're here. Mom and I will buy sandwiches for breakfast."

Our parents follow us to the restaurant as my brothers and I weave through cars and trucks parked near the front door. Red flags are painted on the right-side fenders of three cargo trucks with thirteen stars in the middle of a blue X background.

I ask Dad, "What kind of flag is that?"

His shoulders sag. "They call it Dixie."

"Huh?"

Carrying the baby, Mom pulls Phillip and Charles close to her and grabs my arm.

"Well, son, there's a long story behind that. Right now, I don't want to go into it. I'll just say it's from the Old South during the Civil War."

"That was a long time ago."

Dad breathes in deeply, purses his lips, and blows like he's dousing a candle. "I'll tell you the story some other time..." He glances back at the flag. "When I'm not so tired."

I squint as the diner's door slams shut behind me, wiping my sleepiness away. Hunched over their food at the counter, men look up, nudge one another, and stare, bleary-eyed. Maybe they've never seen six young boys, each a stair-step taller than the other, traipsing past tables to the bathroom. I smile at their sideway looks, but no one smiles back. They don't seem friendly like the folks at home.

Back on the road after leaving that place, I sleep until I hear Dad's cheerful voice. "Wake up, boys. We're in Texas." He sounds excited.

"Texas?" I whisper, looking out at the darkness.

I raise my head above the window rim. Though the sun hasn't risen over the flat landscape, the soft, early desert light silhouettes cactuses, jagged rocks, and miles of parched land. Vivid images of the round diner back in New Mexico, its parking lot, and trucks with the painted Dixie flag swirl through my mind. I pull my jacket over my shoulders to fend off a chill.

"Yep, Texas is the biggest state of the forty-eight!" Dad declares. Even after driving nearly all night, he's still in his usual good mood.

I settle back, eager to finish dreaming about what I have seen on the road.

I wake again as Dad says to Mom, "Route 66 takes us through the Panhandle."

The morning hasn't warmed yet, and the top half of the sun is just peeking above the eastern horizon. Brown tumbleweeds lie still, waiting for the winds to twirl them in unending dances.

During our breakfast stop, somewhere not far off the highway, we sit around a picnic table. Mom packed cold fried chicken for us for breakfast, lunch, and dinner, and it always tastes good, but this morning, we have ham sandwiches she bought at the diner, which are a treat.

I swing my legs back and forth as I study velvety red ants crawling over a dirt mound beneath me. When my family finishes eating and starts to leave, I kick the mound's opening and watch the ants scurry around, looking for their attacker.

* * *

I enjoy the desert's quiet beauty. Like my brothers, I've already gotten more than enough sleep as we drive into the morning sun with the dry wind blasting through our open windows.

Oil derricks pump up and down in wide arcs like hundreds of huge beasts, raising their mosquito-like proboscises and plunging them into the ground as they suck oil with each thrust. The rhythmic movement holds my attention for a while, but as we move on down the road, the scenery soon becomes monotonous.

"Let's sing 'Home on the Range,'" Dad says, and without waiting for us, he starts. We all belt out the song for a few rounds.

"You won't see deer, antelope, or buffalo out here. They don't roam as they once did." He's talkative now that we've eaten and are back on the road. "The correct name for buffalo is bison. I'd like to sing it that way."

We continue with another round, using the word *bison,* which I try to get used to. Then we move on to other tunes that Dad calls negro spirituals. He sings his favorites often.

"Where are we?" Michael asks.

"Texas," Mom and Dad say in unison and then grin at each other.

"Are we ever getting out of Texas?" I ask. "Mom, can we stop and explore some of the places we're passing? That sign..." I don't finish, because we whiz past a poster of a sky-blue waterfall cascading over the words, *Hot Springs.*

"No," Dad replies. "We've gotta keep driving 'til we get to St. Louis."

"How do you stay awake?" I ask.

"I drink a lot of strong, black coffee. The singing helps. As long as I'm singing, I know I'm not sleeping." He winks at me.

"Every time I try to read, I fall asleep." I grumble, and he chuckles.

Mom dampens a cloth for us to wipe our faces, which helps me cool off some. "You need to drink some water," she says, handing me a thermos.

I pass it to my brothers then drain what's left. I still feel thirsty.

In Amarillo, Dad pulls into a gas station with white paint flaking off the siding. Back home, an attendant would hurry out to the car, pump the gas, check the oil, and clean all the windows. But the man in grubby white overalls stands in the doorway next to an old, red soft-drink dispenser and stares blankly as Dad fills the tank and takes care of the car.

With Mom at our heels, we pour out of the car in a hurry to find the restrooms. I lead the way, heading toward the station. The attendant says nothing but watches me like a hawk.

"The bathrooms will be in the back," Mom calls after me.

The unpaved path to the restrooms leads to a door with a sunbaked sign above it, barely clear enough to see the writing: *White*. Mom grabs Phillip's sleeve just before he enters and pulls him to her.

"Don't go in there," she tells him in a tone I've never heard. I look at her with an unasked question on the tip of my tongue.

"The bathroom for kids is over here." She points to an open door a few steps away. It has no hinges and looks like the next strong wind will blow it down.

My brothers rush to the second door. While holding baby Mark, I wait outside with Mom. A sign above that door, just as faint as the other, says *Colored*. Probably the walls of the other one are painted white, and for kids, these are colored.

Charles is the first to file out. "I'm glad I only had to pee."

Each of my brothers follows the other, groaning and holding their noses as they come out. Eager to see what they're reacting to, I go in and notice that someone tried to flush the toilet but the water doesn't empty; it circles like a turd tornado with no place to go other than over the edge. I close my eyes, hold my breath, and urinate quickly before the scum overflows. Like the floor, the walls and sinks are filthy. Since there's no running water, I leave without washing.

The doorway of the white bathroom is ajar. I peek inside as Mom hurries my brothers back to the car. It's clean, and though the toilet looks grimy, it doesn't smell nasty like the one for kids. The path to the toilet and sink is lined with sand and dust, as if someone swept the plank floor only down the middle.

When I go inside the gas station, I find the windows streaked with the same dust that is caked on the sills. Like the restroom floor, a swept path leads to the cash register. Dad is at the counter, paying the glowering attendant.

Once Dad gets back behind the wheel, he scowls as he takes off. No one calls shotgun. The farther away he drives, the more the smell clears from my nose, and I begin to feel better.

"Boy, that place was sickening," says Phillip to no one in particular.

"Yeah. It gave me the creeps." I've never felt so anxious. "Mom, how long will it be before we get out of Texas?"

"I don't know." She doesn't turn to look at me, just looks out her window.

I persist. "I mean how far it is to the Texas border, and what's next?"

"After Texas is Oklahoma, and then we're on to Missouri."

James kneels on his seat. "Mom, are Oklahoma and Missouri far?"

"You kids are too smart for me. It's about three hairs and a freckle."

"Come on, Mom!" James drops back and settles down.

She turns to reach over the seat and tickles him. "Sweetheart, we don't really know. Daddy's had only a few catnaps. He's tired. We still have a long way to go. We'll stop in Oklahoma City for a short rest and then keep going to St. Louis."

"Who are we going to see first when we get to St. Louis?" I ask.

"We're staying with your Uncle Arthur and his family. You'll meet Aunt Ruth and your cousins and see your grandmother. She lives with them. We'll visit my other brothers before we go to Dad's hometown in Mississippi."

"How many brothers do you have?"

"Six."

"And you have six sons. You must love boys," Phillip adds.

"Mom, don't forget Aunt Evelyn," says Michael, leaning across my lap to pop his finger on Phillip's leg.

Phillip pulls back. "She's not her brother. She's a girl." Phillip swats Michael's hand away. "Besides, she lives in Los Angeles, not St. Louis."

"I know where she lives!" Michael shouts.

"Number Three and Number Four, settle down!" Dad says.

"What's gotten into you two?" Mom asks. "Why are you arguing about your Aunt Evelyn?"

"He said she was your brother," Phillip pulls his lips tight.

"No, I didn't."

"Did too."

"Did not."

"You two move over," Mom says.

They scoot away from each other but not far enough, it seems.

"James, give Phillip your seat. And Charles, sit next to Gaylloyd. I want Michael there."

"Why do we have to give up our seats?" James whines but, without waiting for an answer, moves from his window seat.

Charles crawls over me to find his place by the other window. He looks no happier.

"Simmer down, all of you!" Dad says. "I don't want to hear a single peep out of anyone. Understand?"

The sun is deep in the west. Everyone in the car is quiet.

"It's almost dark, George. They're tired," Mom says.

"We're all tired," he says. "Let's pull off on a side road. I need a short nap."

After a few miles, he finds a deserted road and pulls over to shut his eyes for a bit.

"There might be bandits around here," I say to James. "Let's keep a lookout."

OKLAHOMA
7.

I wake when Dad starts the engine. No cowboys, Indians, or robbers bothered us while we slept.

The drive through Texas is long and hot. In Oklahoma, so far, the road moves through grassy lands, sometimes fenced and sometimes not. Everything here is much greener than in the Panhandle, and the wheat and corn fields are more interesting to look at. Most of the time, ours is the only car on the road.

Phillip and Charles kneel on the seat, watching out the windows.

"Daddy, can we stop at an Indian reservation?" Michael asks.

"No. We've got miles to go before we sleep."

James says, "Mom, see those horses?" and crawls over Michael's lap to get a look at the multi-colored animals standing in a fenced pasture far in the distance.

Michael says, "They're just swishing their tails."

"Probably to keep flies from biting," James answers.

Phillip points at them and silently counts.

"What are you doing?" I ask.

"I want to know how many there are."

"Oh! I'll count, too," says Charles, counting aloud.

Phillip stops. "You're mixing me up. Be quiet." Instead, he whinnies and yells at horses in the next field we pass. Some are close to the fence.

"They sure are big," I say.

The first horse I ever saw was in Hawaii. A man brought a brown-and-white pinto to our house. He took my picture on it. I'm wearing a cowboy getup with a hat, chaps, two guns, and a red bandana around my neck. Compared to these horses, the pinto was really small.

"Is your mom my grandma?" Charles asks Dad.

"Yes, my mother was your Grandma Eliza. She and Aunt Myra were sisters. Like many runaway slaves, their mother joined the Choctaws, who lived in the lands between Florida and Mississippi. If you're accepted into the Choctaw tribe, you're a member."

"George, tell them about your grandmother, Big Mama," Mom urges, patting his knee as she smiles back at us. "She was your grandmother's mother."

"I was born in Big Mama's village, Kilmichael, Mississippi. She was still a kid when soldiers raided it, shooting, and killing two of her uncles during the attack. Big Mama lay hidden under their bodies until it was over. After that experience, to save her life from white people, Big Mama lived with other colored tribal members."

Dad's unsmiling reflection shows in the rearview mirror. When he sees me staring at him, he grins broadly.

"You boys look serious. Emma, our sons never heard the word *colored* before. It's a word used around here for negroes." He chuckles.

"I think it's a dumb word," I say. "What color? Red, white, or blue?"

"As far as I'm concerned," James says, "call me black."

"You're not! You're brown."

"Negro is a Spanish word," James says. "Doesn't it mean black?" He nods at us. "Yes! I'm right."

"You're right, James. Well, Grandma Eliza, I'm sad to say, died when my sister was born. I was four—your age. My dad left my sister and me with Aunt Myra, and she raised us. Sister is named after her, but we call her Sissy. We couldn't have two Myras in the same house." He chuckles.

"Where did Grandpa go?" Michael asks. "Why did your dad leave you?"

Dad's voice cracks and his face tightens. "My dad hopped a train to St. Louis to find work. A lot of people left Mississippi in 1914."

"What's *hopping a train*, Daddy?" asks James.

"That's when you ride in one of the train cars that carries boxes and things. Everyone called them boxcars. People rode in one of those if they didn't have any money. Lots of folks did it. They climbed on when the train stopped in their town and hopped off when they got to where they wanted to go, like St. Louis."

I look at Mom, who's wagging her head. "What's wrong, Mom?"

"Well, in those days, many people went to St. Louis for work and sent money to their families, so they could join them," she explains.

"At nineteen," Dad says, "I hopped a train and went to St. Louis to look for my dad. I found him and stayed with him until I finished high school."

Far in the west, the sun is slightly above the horizon.

"You're tuckered out," Mom says to Dad.

"Yeah, I'd like to stop. We're coming into El Reno. It's near Oklahoma City."

"George, I'll keep a lookout for a hotel. We all need baths and a good night's rest. I'll feel better, and tomorrow we'll get an early start."

"And you think we'll find a place in this town? We'll be in and out before you blink your eyes."

"We'll help find one," James offers.

"I'll help," I say.

"Maybe we won't have to sleep in the car," Phillip says. "Let's all look."

Michael asks, "What do we look for?"

On the highway, there are billboards, but not in El Reno. We pass three office buildings right next to one another, then a gas station and two empty wooden shacks in need of paint. They all have signs in dark, printed letters posted in their windows or on the doors, but so small the businesses are difficult to identify. None are hotels, restaurants, or grocery stores.

"There aren't many cars on the streets," I notice.

Several people are on the sidewalk, standing around talking or heading in one direction or another. Only two are negro men, who walk together on our side of the street.

"There's a hotel, Daddy," James cries out, but Dad drives past. His head swivels as he looks at the hotel. "Daddy, didn't you want to stop?"

"How about that restaurant?" Phillip asks.

"There must be a place we can stop for dinner," Mom says. "It'd be nice to have a good hot meal. Pull over, George. I want to ask someone to recommend a place to eat."

"Daddy, there's a lady and her kid." Michael points to a black woman with her hair in a bun, walking ahead of us. She holds the hand of a young, white boy who swoops his arm through air, pretending to fly his blue toy airplane.

Dad stops a short distance ahead of her. She pulls the boy close.

Mom rolls down the window. "Excuse me. We're looking for a restaurant and a place to stay."

"Oh." The woman hesitates then nods to Mom, glances at Dad and the rest of us, and then answers, "Down the road a piece, not far from here, y'all sees some train tracks." She looks back down the street as she speaks. "Once y'all cross 'em, the street becomes dirt. There's a big pistachio tree on the corner, where a yellow house is. Cain't miss it. Y'all make a turn there on your left, and three more houses down is a gray one."

A blue Oldsmobile approaches and slows when it gets near us. The driver and three white women glare at us.

The lady giving directions stops, watching the car until it's out of sight. Then she continues, "Ask fo' Mrs. Tessin. It's her place." She touches Mom's hand. "She helps strangers like y'all."

"Thank you," Mom says. "Your help means so much to us."

The woman keeps hold of the boy's hand as Dad pulls away.

"That's fortunate," he says to Mom. "I wasn't sure we'd find someone to help us."

He turns slowly off the paved road and eases the car into and out of deep potholes, which I find almost funny. I join my brothers' peals of laughter each time Mom's shoulder hits the door. Holding the baby, Michael crashes into Charles. Their giggling is louder than mine.

All the people in this neighborhood are negroes. Some sit and others stand on raised patios, watching the goings-on from their vantage above a walkway. Others stroll on a worn path toward a boardwalk a ways ahead of us. Boardwalks on both sides connect stores facing the road. The last building is a yellow house with a tree in its yard, where the wooden walkway curves out of sight. Business signs on the doors are just as difficult to read as those downtown.

We find Mrs. Tessin's home and pull up alongside the path. The house is a nice wooden bungalow with a white picket fence around it. A stone walkway leads through the yard to stairs that go up to a white door with a small, curtained window.

"Sit quietly while Mom and I talk to the family here," Dad says. "Gaylloyd, you're in charge." Dad and Mom head to the house and knock.

A dark woman opens the door. She's thin and shorter than Mom. Though I hear their voices, I'm unable to make out what they say until they approach the car.

Still chatting and in high spirits, Dad says, "Mrs. Tessin, these are my sons."

She smiles and nods.

"We're staying here," he tells us.

We cheer.

"Johnny Jess's Café is down thataway." Mrs. Tessin points to a single-story building down the road.

"Thank you, ma'am," Dad says. "We'll get a bite to eat and return shortly."

I scramble out of the car last, cross the street, and join Dad and everyone else.

On the boardwalk, James asks, "You don't even know her, and

she's going to let us stay?"

"Then we don't have to pay to stay in a hotel," Phillips says.

"That's not it." Dad looks serious. "We're lucky. There isn't a place around here for... for a big family like ours."

* * *

It's dark by the time we finish dinner. I follow Mom and Dad into a store next to Johnny Jess's Café, where they purchase breakfast makings before we head back. Mr. Tessin helps with the luggage. He doesn't say much but is as hospitable as his wife. They have two small daughters who are already asleep.

"I done made a bed on the floor for your husband and the children," Mrs. Tessin tells Mom.

There are six blankets piled high on top of one another plus pillows—four at the top and three on the other end. On a blanket, head to toe, we will look like sardines.

"James, Dad, and me at one end," I say, "with Michael, Phillip, Charles, and the baby at our feet."

"Y'all sleep on the sofa, Emma," Mrs. Tessin says to Mom.

She sighs. "I'm tired, but I want Mark to sleep with me."

I look at the couch. "That's a sofa?"

"I can imagine y'all looking forward to hot baths," Mrs. Tessin says. "I'll get the tub ready. Who's first?"

Mom and Mrs. Tessin wash and dry the two youngest, while Dad takes care of Phillip and Michael. James bathes before me. We are old enough to take care of ourselves, and I feel great, soaking alone in the tub. The warm water and soap bubbles almost lull me to sleep, until I remember how tired Mom and Dad are and hurry to finish, so they can take their baths.

The floor is hard, but all those blankets make it pretty comfortable, and I can stretch out to my full length, which feels much better than sleeping in the car.

Early the next morning, I join Dad in the kitchen. "I talked to Mrs. Tessin about cooking breakfast," he tells me.

She watches from the doorway, as I remove toast from the oven.

"I'm not making much," he assures her, "just fixin' flapjacks, sausage, fried eggs, hash browns, and toast—enough to feed an army. I'm sure y'all will enjoy it." I don't hear him use the Southern dialect often, but he seems to enjoy it. "I don't get much chance for down-home talk in California," he says.

"Y'all sound fine to me, and I'm right pleased y'all's fixin' breakfast," Mrs. Tessin says. Her two daughters, six and eight, appear behind her, still in their night clothes and rubbing their eyes.

"Hello," the taller one says to me. "What's your name?"

"Gaylloyd." I'm amazed at how bashful I feel.

"Gaylord?" their mom asks.

"No, Gaylloyd." I raise my voice to emphasize *Lloyd.* "It's not lord."

"What kinda name is that?" she asks Dad. "It's not a Christian name."

"He's my oldest son. I gave him the names of two buddies killed in the war."

"*Hmm,*" Mrs. Tessin says.

I'd never thought about how I got my name. I'll have to talk to Dad more about that.

After breakfast, James and I wash dishes and help pack the car. Just before I get in, Dad hands Mrs. Tessin three five-dollar bills. "Thank you for putting up with us."

She grabs his hand and crumples the money back into his palms. "George, I didn't ask for anything, but I have something for you. It'll be quite helpful." She hands him a magazine. "You may not have heard of this book in California. My family uses it all the time. It's *The Negro Travelers' Green Book.*"

ST. LOUIS, MISSOURI

8.

"**S**on, hold this guide," Dad says, handing the booklet to me. "I'll take a look at it at our next rest stop."

The green cover page shows a four-lane freeway interchange. Below the title, *The Negro Traveler's' Green Book*, is its description, *A Guide for Travel and Vacations*.

After looking at the first two pages, I say to him, "It's old—from twenty years ago." I turn the page. "Here's a list of the states, and Missouri is on page thirty-three." There it has a list of the state's cities, including St. Louis. In the middle of the page is a hotel advertisement. "Dad, there's a list of restaurants and places we can stay."

"Well, that's fine," he says, "but we won't need it now. We'll be at your uncle's in no time."

Mom shakes her head slightly. "George, not quite that soon. It's going to take us several hours before we arrive."

As we cross the border, beneath a cloud-free, blue sky, a billboard welcomes us. Missouri's warm air sticks to my skin. I'm sure it's an omen of the temperature for our stay at our first home away from home.

"We'll stop for lunch in Springfield," Dad says. "Find Springfield in the *Green Book*. Does it recommend a restaurant, Gaylloyd?

"Six."

"I'll stop at a gas station and get directions."

"Dad, there are two places to go for gas."

We find one of them, a clean Esso station like the ones at home, with its familiar red logo on a white background. A negro attendant meets Dad before he can get out of the car.

"Yes sir," he says. "Is it a fill up?"

Dad says yes, shows him the *Green Book*, and asks for directions to one of the restaurants.

* * *

After lunch, my stomach flutters as if butterflies are bumping around inside. To calm myself, I sit behind Dad and watch the flat landscape. There are some wooden houses far back from the roadside with single hickory, oak, or maple trees in front of many of them. Cars speed past us. The scenery holds my interest less and less the closer we get to St. Louis.

"See those kids?" Michael asks. "They're playing with their dog."

"What's so important about them playing with their dog?" says Phillip.

Michael reaches forward and taps Mom on the shoulder. "Do our cousins have a dog?"

"I don't think so," she says.

He's not the only one thinking about what we can expect during our visit. "I hope Grandma will take us to see the Cardinals," I say to James. "She and I love baseball."

The last time she visited San Diego, we sat around the radio in the living room and listened to the game.

"Grandma promised she'll have tickets. I hope she hasn't forgotten," I added.

"I'm sure she hasn't," Mom says. "While we're in St. Louis, we'll see all my brothers and your dad's stepmother."

I pull my sweaty T-shirt up over my sticky stomach and flap

the edges, trying to cool myself. The Texas Panhandle may have been hotter, but here, the muggy air makes me complain, as if someone could change it.

Six hours pass, until the sun nearly sets on the horizon and the air feels cooler. We enter a neighborhood of stately trees with arched branches that form green tunnels to my uncle's house.

"Wow, look at those sidewalks!" Groomed lawns and curved paths lead to the front door of each impressive brick home. "I almost can't believe I lived here my whole first year," I say to my brothers.

Dad slows the Packard to a stop just short of the driveway leading to a rust-red brick house with white shutters next to the windows. Over the front door, carved wood looks like goats' horns. Dad and Mom climb out of the car before we do.

Standing on the walkway with his hands on his hips, Dad twists and stretches backward as he looks at Uncle Arthur's home. "This house is elegant."

I nudge Mom's arm. "I love brick. I want to have a brick house just like this when I'm grown."

My brothers stand right next to me, looking at the neighborhood around us. Mom wraps her arms around Mark, but he pushes back on her shoulders so he can look. Dad leads us to the door, where we huddle together as he rings the bell.

I haven't seen my uncles in a long time. James, Michael, and I are the only ones who've met them, though I believe Michael was too small to remember.

Aunt Ruth answers the door.

Mom's voice breaks our silence. "We're here!"

"Welcome! Welcome!" Her eyes sparkle as she greets us. She looks pregnant. Her eyeglasses and short-cropped, dark hair give her an intellectual look. Her very pale skin means she hasn't been lying around in the sun.

"Please, come in. Grandma hasn't returned from her outing yet." Looking back into the house, she says breathlessly, "My kids are somewhere around here. I think Paul and Peter are in the back yard. Mary and Maggie are in the living room with their dad.

Lettie's in the kitchen. We're getting dinner ready. You must be famished. How was your trip? Arthur, they're here! Come in, come in."

She brushes each of my cheeks with a kiss as soon as I step inside. Dad follows all of us, but she ignores him, not giving him so much as a look, never mind a double kiss on the cheeks. There's an edginess between my aunt and dad.

I enter the soft-white living room. A dark-blue carpet fills the floor like an ocean and then surges up a curved staircase. Paintings of flowers I've never seen before hang on every wall. Uncle Arthur and two of his daughters play with blocks and other toys. Their games look messy, but everything else in the room is neat.

My other cousins burst into the room all at once.

"Quiet down and listen to your mother," Uncle Arthur says to them. "Everyone has waited a long time for this moment." He seems to be talking to my brothers and me as well as his own kids. "Go ahead, Ruth."

We gawk at one another while Aunt Ruth introduces us. Then, she tells Mom, "The children will sleep upstairs. There are four bedrooms and a bathroom on the second floor." To her sons standing beside me, she adds, "Paul and Peter, help your cousins put their things away."

Like James and me, they're fourteen months apart. I'm a year older than Paul, but we're the same height. Paul's Coke-bottle-thick glasses emphasize his slim stature.

"Follow me," Paul blurts out.

We go to the car and grab our suitcases, then the four of us bound up the stairs to a bedroom with a sash window next to a back door. Paul opens the door and leads us into the screened-in porch overlooking the backyard.

Paul gestures to two queen-size beds with almost no space between them. "This is where we're sleeping."

I extend my arms into a T and drop on the bed closest to the window then flap my arms like I'm making a sand angel. James falls next to me, and our cousins join us. We squeal and laugh as we jump from one bed to the other.

Lettie leads Phillip onto the porch, and they stand in the doorway watching us. Phillip seems to have attached himself to her. She's stylish like her mom, but doesn't wear glasses. Her dark hair falls past her shoulders and bounces as she walks. She's not pudgy like some girls in my seventh-grade class.

"Paul, Mom isn't going to be happy with you guys jumping on the beds," she says, looking at me.

Phillip puts on his determined look.

"We're not hurting anything," James says and bounces harder onto the other bed.

"We better do as she says," I tell James, scooting off the bed and sliding onto the floor. I know Phillip will call Dad if we don't stop. Lettie leads Phillip back to the room where Michael unpacks, paying no attention to us.

Looking down, I see that the yard is grassy but without trees. A swing set moves slightly in the breeze, and a short, covered, wooden box sits in one corner. Behind the back fence runs an alley.

"What's inside that thing?" I ask, pointing to the structure.

"Oh, that? It's just a sandbox," says Paul. "My kid sisters play in it all the time. Dad covers it at night to keep cats from burying poop in it." He steps away from the screen. "Follow me. I'll show you the basement."

Going back through the room, I call to Michael and Phillip, "Leave your stuff and come with us." As Paul points out the bathroom across the hall, I urge Michael, "Come on. We're going downstairs with Paul. He's showing us around."

We skip the main section of the house and follow him into the basement, which is one massive room the same size as the first floor. Right away, I notice a musty oil smell. There's not much light at the far end, but I can make out a white washing machine against an unpainted gray wall and five clothes lines hanging from the ceiling. One has four pairs of trousers hanging on it and a basket of clothes beneath it, as if someone stopped in the midst of hanging them.

Right in the middle of the basement is a large, rectangular, metal box with a stove pipe that disappears into the ceiling. Near it, the oil smell gets more pungent. On the room's other side are three open windows near the far corner, where a door with a small, circular window lets sunlight stream onto the concrete floor. The door opens to the back yard.

"Look!" says James. "A ping-pong table."

Phillip stands next to him, looking at another table behind them that holds a complete electric train set with people, houses, and trees.

Charles and Maggie, who are almost the same age, come down to join us, leaving the door ajar. The doorbell rings, and I hear the door open.

"I saw a new car parked in front," an old woman says. "Arthur, have they arrived yet?"

We all look at one another.

"*Grandma!*" I shout.

"*Grandma!*" Paul screams and charges up the stairs. The rest of us scramble after him.

GRANDMA

9.

Running up the stairs isn't quick enough to satisfy my eagerness to see Grandma. I pause at the top. When she sees me and smiles, my spirit brightens. Still holding several bags, she embraces Mom. All the kids storm past me and gather around her. Even with the front door still open, the vestibule is as crowded and boisterous as when we arrived.

"You're a sight for sore eyes," she tells Mom, their tears mingling where their faces meet. Grandma pulls back and takes a better look at her daughter. "You finally made it here." She dabs moisture from her cheeks with the back of her hand.

Uncle Arthur greets his mother. "How was your trip?"

"It was quick. All I could think about was getting home to see everyone. You'd think I'd been gone a month of Sundays instead of just a few hours."

Mom looks down and sees Mark crawling on his hands and knees as fast as he can to keep up with the rest of us kids. He pulls himself up by her skirt hem, and she lifts him into her arms.

"This is Mark," says Dad as he comes in from the living room. "He was born last year, three days after Gaylloyd's birthday."

"Well, hello, George. I didn't see you come in," says Grandma.

"I was outside looking around. It's been a long time since I've been in this city. I've had a lot of hard times here and a lot of good ones, too."

"It couldn't have been too bad," jokes Mom. "We met in this town!"

"Thank God for that!"

Uncle Arthur tells his son, "Paul, put Grandma's bags in her room."

Paul takes as many as he can carry, and I take the rest. They're not heavy. We leave them in Grandma's lavender-scented bedroom, just off the main hallway.

When we come back, the other children are leading Grandma into the living room. "I'll sit on the couch," she says, making herself comfortable. "All of you sit right here next to me. Gaylloyd, I need that bag here." She points to one next to her purse. Mom puts Mark on her lap, and everyone else jockeys for a position close to Grandma.

Mark looks at her face and strokes her cheek. She nuzzles him nose-to-nose. "Mark certainly looks like his mama, Emma," Grandma gushes and Mom beams.

The shelves near the grand piano are laden with sheet music and many music books. Dad sits on the piano bench and compliments Aunt Ruth. "I like the way you have your piano positioned in the middle of the room."

"George, where do you keep yours?" asks Aunt Ruth.

"Close to the living room window."

"A piano should never be by a window. The cold is bad for it!"

"That may be true here, but in San Diego, it rarely gets cold."

"Aha! Emma and I are going to get dinner ready," exclaims Aunt Ruth, nodding to Grandma.

Dad and my aunt have always been rivals, especially about music. She's a classically trained music teacher, and Dad is mostly self-taught. He told me he once wanted to be a concert pianist.

Grandma says, "I have something for everyone." She pulls her bag close and takes stock of how many of us are sitting around. Beginning with Mark, she hands an unwrapped gift to each child, from youngest to oldest. I'm the eldest cousin, next to Lettie, I have the longest wait, which doesn't seem fair! "Gaylloyd, look at how much you've grown. You're almost a man!"

I squirm with a mixture of anxiety, pleasure, and self-consciousness. Peter and Paul waste no time razzing me. "Yup, he's got a mustache."

"Shush now," Grandma admonishes. "You boys will be grown soon enough! All my grandkids are becoming fine young women and men." I admire the way she treats girls and boys as equals.

Mark hugs his new black-and-white panda bear in his chubby arms. It's half his size. He explores its eyes and ears, which makes Grandma smile.

Aunt Ruth peeks out from the kitchen door. "Lettie, I need your help."

With a new book from Grandma in hand, Lettie steps over Maggie and Charles, who are lying on the floor, playing with their new toys.

I blurt out, "Aunt Ruth, what's for dinner?"

Lettie answers before her mother has a chance to respond, "Peppers baked with ground meat. It's an Italian dish with special seasonings. I'm helping fix it." Her face brightens as she skips away. In Aunt Ruth's home, I've noticed the girls help in the kitchen. In our home, my brothers and I help cook. I guess some things are good about an all-boy household.

"I know you'll enjoy this," Grandma says, handing me a copy of Rudyard Kipling's *Just So Stories* with an eye-catching cover. Her choice is perfect for me. She knows I love animals, science, and nature.

"Grandma, thanks!" I kiss her on the cheek then thumb through its strange stories. The first one to pop out is "How the Whale Got His Throat." Looking up from the book, I ask, "When are you coming back to visit us in California?" Years have gone by since she stayed at our house.

She chuckles. "Child, I'm getting old. I won't be able to take a train out to San Diego again. The last time I traveled across the country, it almost killed me." Holding her chin with her thumb and index finger, she seems to study me. "That time I came out to see you," she continues, twisting her lips, "it was after your return from

Hawaii. Your Mama was pregnant with Charles." She smiles at him.

"My train stopped in Del Mar." Grandma takes Peter's hand into hers. "It's a small village not far north of San Diego. It was early morning, still dark when I got off the coach for a moment to buy nuts. I didn't take long at all in the station, paying for my snack, but I got back just in time to see the train pull away."

When Grandma puts her head down, I realize this embarrasses her. Without looking at us, she describes what she did next in a softer voice. "I panicked. I climbed off the platform and chased the train down the rails! I kept falling over my own feet. The gravel bloodied my hands and knees and tore my stockings.

"When I got off the tracks, I made my way to the coastal highway by the ocean. I didn't realize how far I was from San Diego, so I just kept walking along that road. I usually love the smell of the salty air blowing off the water, but it wasn't calming at that time. Walking was difficult wearing shoes like these." She lifts her skirt and shows us her black, ankle-high lace-ups with blocky heels.

"Granny shoes!" Paul says.

I choke back a laugh.

Grandma scowls at him. "Anyway, I had several twenty-dollar bills with me and waved them in the air, attempting to flag someone down. The kindest Filipino couple gave me a lift to your house. I was surprised when they refused to take any money. They said, 'It's the Christian thing to do.'"

She gazes toward the kitchen. "Whatever they're cooking in there sure smells good!" Then she continues her story. "Your Aunt Emma scolded me for taking such a big chance," she tells my cousins. "She said crooks could have knocked me out, robbed me, and left me for dead by the side of the road." Her eyes look watery.

"You could have called us," Dad says. "I would have come to get you."

"I couldn't think of what else to do at the time," she says.

Dad nods. "Mother, this won't be our last time to come to see you."

"Are we going to see Grandpa?" James asks. He and I are the only ones old enough to remember seeing him before we left for Hawaii. I must have been about four and remember only a few things about him.

"I don't think your mama told you your grandpa is gone," Grandma says, "because you were so small. Papa died two years after I got back home from San Diego." She glances at Dad, who bows his head, then turns to James, "Your Grandpa Burgette grew up in Chariton County, Missouri. Back in those days, it was a German settlement. You may not have learned in school yet about the War Between the States, but one reason for the Civil War was to abolish slavery."

"What's that, Grandma?" Michael asks.

She stares at the ceiling as if searching for a good answer. "Slavery is when people are forced to work for nothing and are not allowed to do anything without permission. Chariton was an abolitionist town. They didn't believe in slavery."

"What's abolitionist, Grandma?" interrupts James.

Grandma looks at Dad, who says, "Mother, it's okay."

"Abolitionists were people who believed it's not right to force someone to work with no pay. They often bought slaves and freed them. That's how Grandpa's family came to be free."

"You mean Grandpa's family was in slavery?" I ask.

"Your Grandpa was born free ten years after the Civil War, but his parents were born into slavery and stayed slaves until the abolitionists freed them. He grew up in Germantown, where the whole town spoke German."

"I've heard you and your sister talking in French," Dad says. "Can you speak German?"

"No. In St. Joe, people spoke pawpaw, a kind of Creole French. Although no one sees us as Cherokees, our family traded with the French long before the English came." She breaks her train of thought and looks around. "I didn't leave my parents' home until after Papa…" She nods at my cousins sitting on the floor. "After Grandpa and I married."

I glance at my brothers and cousins. They're not playing with their gifts, because, like me, they are paying close attention to what she's telling us.

"My family owned a plantation near St. Joe," she says.

"A plantation, Grandma?" I ask.

Dad says, "You'll see a few when we get to Mississippi."

Grandma continues her story. "They were like farms where the workers lived and took care of the property. A few Indians owned plantations and ran them like the French did. The Cherokees were no different. My father used to tell me how our people, the Wolf Clan, owned slaves to help develop the plantation where I grew up. We grew corn, beans, and squash to feed ourselves, and hops for making beer. Dad was one of the Black Indian soldiers who fought for Lincoln. He had a hard time, because he spoke only French and Tsalagi Gawonihisdi, plus a few words of English."

The way Grandma relates the Cherokee side of our family impresses me. I wonder why Mom never talks about it.

"When Grandpa and I first met, we couldn't understand each other." She chuckles. "Our languages were so different, and we didn't want our children to struggle like we did. We wanted them to have a better life than we'd had. We decided to speak only English at home, which was a struggle for Grandpa. With his business friends, he always spoke German."

At a loss for words, everyone sits quietly and listens to laughing voices from the kitchen mingle with the aromas of garlic, onions, and tomatoes. "Dinner's ready!" Lettie calls.

My mouth waters. "Grandma, are you hungry?"

Michael answers for her. "We're starved!" Everyone scrambles up and hurries into the dining room.

The long walnut table is covered with a white-lace tablecloth and vase of fresh flowers, and is loaded with dishes of roasted stuffed peppers, steaming rice, and sliced carrots. I sit next to Uncle Arthur. For years, I've seen his picture hanging on the wall at home alongside other relatives, but he's so much more handsome in person. He's tall, like Dad. His cheeks remind me of fresh, roasted chestnuts and blend with his smile.

When we are all in our places, Uncle Arthur bows his head and blesses the meal.

Gabbing and laughter flood the room. Uncle Arthur hands me the hollandaise sauce for my stuffed pepper and asks, "Do you play badminton?"

"Is that a board game?"

Peter laughs out loud and chokes on his food.

Uncle Arthur nods in an understanding way. "It's a racquet game, something like tennis. We're playing Saturday."

Peter hasn't stopped chuckling.

I ask, "Why Saturday? What are we doing tomorrow?"

From across the table, Dad says, "We're visiting your Great-Uncle Jack, Grandma's youngest brother." Always quick to compliment, he adds, "Ladies, this is delicious! Ruth, I want your recipe for this stuffed pepper dish."

Aunt Ruth smiles. "It's something my mother often made for my father and me when we lived in Milan. She taught me everything I know about cooking."

Phillip asks, "Milan?"

"In Italy," Lettie explains. "That's where Mother was born."

With a mouth full of spicy sausage, I ask, "How did you and Uncle Arthur meet? Was it in Italy?"

Mom gives me a sharp look. "Gaylloyd, how many times have I asked you not to talk with food in your mouth?"

"No, in church here in St. Louis, where I sing," my uncle says. "Your aunt is the organist."

Aunt Ruth says, "I was only twelve when my father and I left Italy. Lots of people fled to get away from Mussolini. Because of him, my mother was killed."

"How was she killed?" Phillip furrows his brow.

Dad looks hard at my naïve brother. "Phillip, I don't think that's something she wants to talk about."

"George, he's only seven." Aunt Ruth smiles at Phillip. "My father refuses to talk to me, so I really don't know what happened. People at home were frightened and kept a lot of secrets."

My thoughts meld the stories of Grandma and Aunt Ruth with the ones Dad told us while we were on the road. I'm not sure what to think about everything. My family history is more complicated than anything I've learned in school. I glance at Mom, who's sitting next to Dad. I wonder if she knows how confused I feel.

She smiles at me. "Mama, Gaylloyd was so cute when he was three, and he heard a radio story giving thanks to Americans for their sacrifices during World War II. He wondered what that meant, so I told him about how nylons, soap, and sugar were rationed. I showed him a book of the ten-cent defense stamps. I explained how I was worried about my brothers fighting in Germany, but he was so young, I didn't think he understood. Then he says," and she mimics my high voice, "'Mom, Grandpa is German. Your brothers had nothing to worry about. Hitler wouldn't have killed them. They have German blood!'" She looks at me again. "You were so serious then."

"And you haven't changed a bit." Grandma nods toward Mom, and they giggle.

I stand and lift my shoulders, hoping to appear more grown up. "Aunt Ruth, I know nothing about Mussolini or why your father wouldn't tell you about what happened to your mother. And Grandma, I don't understand why our family had slaves. Mom has never told me anything about the Wolf Clan and their plantations."

Mom frowns at me and shakes her head then fidgets with her hair, removing a bobby pin and laying it next to her plate. Seldom have I seen her nervous.

My end of the table is quiet, and none of the adults are eating. There's a hum of conversation at the other end of the table, where the younger kids are too busy eating to listen to me. I look to Dad for an answer.

"There are a lot of things Mom and I will tell you later, son. This just isn't the time."

I guess I'll just have to wait until the right moment. Self-conscious about my tone of voice with the grown-ups, I realize how quiet it is, so I sit down.

"Is there dessert, Aunt Ruth?" Michael asks as he plays with the fork on his empty plate.

Dad smiles and nods. "Time to desert the table!" My cousins

laugh. My siblings and I don't, having heard Dad's stale old joke many times before. Dad seems pleased with himself.

"There's no dessert, honey," Aunt Ruth says. "You children are excused from the table." As Lettie and I stand, she says, "I would like you and Gaylloyd to clear the table and wash the dishes."

Mom watches me pick up several plates to take to the kitchen. "Be careful with your aunt's dinnerware."

"Okay, Mom." Like a waiter, I place the next one atop the others.

A pocket door separates the dining room from the kitchen. The pale blue-and-white tones of the walls and floor match counters that are decorated with blue birds. I set the dishes on the tiled countertop and fill the sink with hot, soapy water. I peer out the three-paned window, but it's too dark to see the back yard.

"If you don't mind, I'll wash and you dry," I suggest to Lettie, and she agrees.

We can still hear the adult conversation in the dining room, where Grandma's talking to Mom and Uncle Arthur. "Your papa was a good man. His death came as a surprise. He was so healthy, no one was expecting it. He had just decided to retire and sold the butcher shop we'd kept open even during the Depression."

"I would have liked my children to have known him," Mom says. "Gaylloyd and James were the only ones who met him, but they were so small then. I'm not sure what they remember about him."

Aunt Ruth nods. "Yeah, I know. He's the only grandpa my children knew. My father wasn't at our wedding and hasn't seen any of our children. I was pregnant with Paul the last time I saw him. I did have lunch with him, hoping he'd accept that I married the man I love. Maybe someday my prayers will be answered."

I give the last clean plate to Lettie, and then we return to the dining room.

GERMAN

10.

Grandma takes my hand and pats the couch next to her, where she wants me to sit. "What do you remember about your grandpa? You were his favorite, I think, because you were his first grandson."

"I remember him carrying me on his shoulders, talking to me all the time. I'm sure it was in German. I can tell you a story he told me when I was a kid."

Dad and Uncle Arthur burst into laughter. "When you were a kid?"

Grandma snaps at them, "You two stop it, now." She turns back to me. "Just ignore them, honey."

I think about sticking my tongue out at them, but instead say to Grandma, "Well, he taught me how to count. Every time I got a chance, I'd ask him to repeat his story about a man selling eggs."

"Yeah, I know that one." Uncle Arthur smirks. "Go ahead and tell us."

"It's in German," I remind everyone. "A woman and her son entered an egg market. '*Guten Morgen, meine Frau. Wie geht es ihnen?*' the egg seller said."

I check to see if Lettie is listening but can't tell if she understands. "The translation is, 'Good morning, my lady. How are you today?'" She knew Grandpa, and he probably spoke to her in

German, too, but I want to impress her.

"'*Guten Morgen*. I need two dozen eggs,' the woman told the clerk.

"'Of course. I'll be happy to count them for you. *Eins, zwei, drei, vier, fünf frische Eier…*' One, two, three, four, five fresh eggs," I add.

"This egg-seller always made small talk when he was helping customers. He asked the woman, 'How old is your son, *miene Frau?*'

"'*Dreizeh*,' she answered.

"'*Vierzehn, fünfzehn, sechzehn,*' he continued. Fourteen, fifteen, sixteen.

"'And your husband?' he asked. 'I'm trying to remember how long you told me you'd been married?'

"'*Zwanzig Jahre*,' she replied.

"'*Einundzwanzig,   zweiundzwanzig,   dreiundzwanzig, vierundzwanzig frische Eier…*' Twenty-one, twenty-two, twenty-three, twenty-four fresh eggs.

"'There you go, all counted out for you,' he said and handed her the bag."

"'Oh, you're so helpful.' Then, the woman paid for twenty-four eggs and waved as she walked away from the egg stand." When I finish, I slouch back onto the couch.

"That's a funny story," Lettie says.

"It's my favorite."

"That's one of Grandpa's best ones," Dad says. "I studied German at San Diego Community College. But my father-in-law, your grandpa, died before I could impress him."

Lettie stares quietly at me and smiles. "So, the lady bought only a dozen eggs."

"Yes! Good," her father praises her. "I only picked up a few German words from your grandpa. Are you two finished cleaning up?"

We nod.

"Go on upstairs. With so many people here, I want you kids to start getting ready for bed now. Tell everyone it's almost bedtime. Lettie, make sure your sisters get in their pj's and brush their teeth.

Gaylloyd, you and Paul will take care of the boys. Your dad and I will be up soon to tuck you in and listen to your prayers."

Long after they checked on us, our cousins and James and I are still awake, telling funny family stories. We try to be quiet, but now and then, we erupt into raucous giggles. Paul and Peter know all our relatives in St. Louis and tell us a lot about Great-Uncle Jack, who seems to have made a big impression on them.

Paul tells me, "He lives on a farm."

"You won't believe the size of it until you get there." Peter spreads his arms as far back as his shoulders allow.

Mouth agape, I lean back against the bed's headboard. "Do you think it's like the cattle ranches we saw in Texas?"

"Yeah, but he doesn't have cattle. He has horses, racing horses," Paul adds.

James says, "You should have seen the huge horses in Oklahoma! I think they're the same ones they use in the movies."

The sandman pours sand in our eyes and soon our stories drift off into sleep.

MOM'S BROTHERS AND GREAT-UNCLE JACK

11.

"Your Uncle Arthur is at work at Ma Bell," Aunt Ruth tells me during breakfast. Because, like Mom, she doesn't drive, she and the kids are stranded without Uncle Arthur, so our cousins don't come with us to visit the rest of Mom's brothers.

"Grandma, everyone's ready." I hold the Packard's rear door open and help her into the car.

We all say at once, "Sit here, Grandma. Sit here!" And we jostle to make space for her.

The car's rumbling engine echoes our thrill to meet Grandma's youngest brother and more of Mom's brothers. Dad will also meet them for the first time.

On our way to Uncle Gus's, Mom tells us his house shares walls with neighbors on either side and they have no front yard. "It's a row house," she says.

Dad parks next to two other cars in a nearby lot bordered by a short masonry wall. The sidewalks on both sides of the street are well cared for. It's treeless but clean. With smiles, stretching from ear to ear, Uncle Gus and his wife stand on a landing above the steps with their front door wide open. Uncle Gus is neither stocky nor slim and wears black slacks and a white, short-sleeved shirt. He's taller than his wife. She's wearing a yellow dress.

I climb the steps ahead of my brothers, followed by Mom and Dad. All over Uncle Gus's face are tiny black bumps like freckles, but they're disturbing. My aunt's dark hair is neatly arranged in a low bun. She's light-skinned and slimmer than Mom.

"Howdy," Uncle Gus says. "Been expectin' you, been expectin' you."

The aroma of something sweet welcomes me as I step inside Uncle Gus's house.

Echoing him, my aunt says to my brothers, "Howdy, folks. It's good to see y'all. I'm Ida Mae. Aunt Ida Mae to y'all. I hope y'all like cookies. Just out of the oven. Oatmeal. Can y'all smell 'em?"

"We sure can," comes the chorus of replies from everyone except Grandma.

Aunt Ida Mae leads us past a set of stairs near her front door into the living room, where cookies about the size of my hand are stacked on a platter. "There's a lot of raisins in ma cookies. I hope y'all like 'em."

With a cookie in hand, I settle on a lumpy, gray couch between my brothers. The living room couch faces another room, set up with a card table with a deck of cards on it and four chairs, one on each side. Uncle Gus leads Grandma and my folks to the table.

Dozens of framed photos are displayed on the walls in the living room where we sit, crowded together. Phillip gets up to go look at them, followed by the rest of us. The pictures are of my grandparents, Mom, her siblings, and other people I don't know, maybe relatives.

In the card room is a glass cabinet showcasing dozens of bottles in myriad colors, shapes, and sizes.

"This is my liquor room," Uncle Gus says to Dad.

"We don't keep the stuff in the house because of the kids," Dad replies.

"We just had breakfast," says Mom, who sounds surprised that he sets a drink in front of her.

"I know you likes Old Fashions, Emma." He laughs with a mischievous grin. "I had four whisky sours before you got here.

That's my breakfast."

Dad takes a drink from him, and Grandma says she wants the same thing as Aunt Ida Mae. Mom watches as the other four noisily play bid whist, a card game. Uncle Gus says something funny to Dad, who almost falls off his chair. Grandma looks at the ceiling and shakes her head at Uncle Gus.

Mom leaves the room and walks over to me, biting her bottom lip. "Gus!" she shouts, "I don't want my children hearing that type of talk."

He laughs harder. "You know it's funny."

"What's so funny?" I ask, but no one answers. The family photographs are interesting, and my cookie's good, but I'm getting antsy, sitting around. This is not my idea of having fun.

After a few minutes, a tall, skinny boy about my age comes in and sits on the couch.

"Hi. Y'all wanna see the back yard?" he asks.

"Sure," we answer all at once.

Going downstairs, he blurts, "I'm adopted."

"Okay," I'm puzzled about why he's telling me, especially since I don't know him and didn't even know he was in the house.

"Do you care?"

"Do I care about what?"

"I'm not your blood kin. Does it matter to you?"

"No."

He smiles. "I'm glad. My name's Benj."

The yard outside is paved and enclosed by a wooden fence. Dead weeds fill cracks crisscrossing the pavement. Near a black '49 Ford truck, a bicycle sits upside down on its handlebars. Pliers and a screwdriver lie on the ground below. Benj picks up his tools and spins the bike's front wheel. "I was working on my bike. I didn't know what time you guys were coming, so I came inside to get a cookie and see if you were here yet."

James stands on the running board of the truck. On the ground beside the hood , five tires are stacked up, all way too big for the truck.

"I pretend I'm a truck driver," Benj says. "Let's get inside and play we're going to Gram's."

He slides in behind the steering wheel, and my brothers scramble in, scooting close together to make room. I climb on the tires, look around the yard, and try to see over the fence. There's nothing much to see other than his neighbor's fence on the other side of the alley.

Grandma steps out the back door. "Boys, come back inside."

My brothers tumble out of the truck one at a time and head inside. I lie on my stomach, figuring a way to slide down the tire mountain.

Standing nearby and waiting for me to climb off, Benj says, "Hello, Grams."

"Grams! I ain't your grandma. Nobody calls me Grams."

Benj pushes his way past her into the house, bumping her. I hear him run upstairs and slam a door. Grandma scowls.

Uncle Gus storms into the yard. "Aw, Mama, he knows he's adopted. I want you to treat him like he's your own grandchild. Won't you do that?"

"No, I can't."

Uncle Gus looks up to Benj's open window and calls, "Benj, come on down, son."

I hear loud sobs as we go inside. Aunt Ida Mae climbs the stairs and knocks on a shut door. "Come out when you want to, son," she says gently, then comes back down.

This is the first time I've ever heard Grandma say anything unkind.

"Mama, you know we've always wanted a child," Aunt Ida Mae says once she reaches us. "We tried to have one of our own, but God works in mysterious ways. After a few years, Benj came into our lives, and we're raising him just like our own. He needs a grandma."

"I know all about his mother and can't be his grandma. I won't forget what her life is."

"Yeah, we know, but Mama, she has nothing to do with him. He's a good boy. Adopting unfortunate children is the Christian thing to do."

Grandma scoffs. "Well, true or not, I can't love him and that's final."

I'm surprised to realize that Grandma doesn't love him because of his mother. Being in our family is obviously important to Benj. I follow her to the living room and join my brothers, who are all bunched together on the couch. She continues on to the liquor room and sits at the card table with Mom and Aunt Ida Mae.

I grab another cookie and pick up a magazine from the coffee table. I've never seen anything like it and show it to my brothers.

James takes a look. "What's that?"

I show him the cover of *Ebony* then thumb through it. I've never seen a magazine showing so many negro people. On every page, the people are negroes, *even in the advertisements*. The stories are about negroes, including one with a photograph of a minister standing at a pulpit, his right arm raised. The caption says *Reverend Martin Luther King Jr*. I study the picture. When I realize the church is not Catholic, I lose interest and hand it to James. I smell cigarette smoke, which I'm not used to. Dad and Aunt Ida Mae are smoking.

"George, I think it's time to mosey down the road a piece. We have a lot of people to see," Mom says.

"Okay, you guys. Let's go," I say to my brothers.

Dad says to Uncle Gus and Aunt Ida Mae, "It's good to have finally met you two."

Aunt Ida Mae picks up Dad's untouched glass. Mom's has lipstick on it, but most of her drink is still in it. Grandma's is empty.

As we leave, I walk by Uncle Gus, who slurs, "Goo' weye," and sways against Aunt Ida Mae, who is standing on the porch next to him. I'm sure he refilled his glass many times.

In the car, I look back as we drive away. Aunt Ida Mae is already inside.

* * *

Our next stop is at Uncle Clyde's, another brother Mom wants to see. The smell of his newly cut lawn welcomes us to his small house.

His wife, Aunt Donie looks surprised, as though she's forgotten we were coming. "Clyde's at work," she tells Grandma.

I sip the orange soda my aunt gives me. Mom and Dad ask for coffee.

After Grandma introduces us, she says, "Donie, I'm sorry Clyde isn't here, because Emma is staying only a few more days. I wonder if the main reason Grandma wants to visit here is to remind them of the ball game.

Our visit is short. Soon, Mom says as she stands up, "Boys, it's time to head out. We have a few more stops to make."

I'm not the only one to perk up and jump to my feet.

"We'll see you at the game," Grandma says to Donie, adding, "I brought you a little something," and hands her a gift from her bag.

* * *

After we've been on the road for more than an hour, we reach Uncle Lyman's in Brentwood. Dad slowly drives up a long, tree-lined driveway to his house. A Jaguar and two Mercedes are parked in front.

Mom's oldest brother, Lyman, is a doctor. His Humpty Dumpty stomach stretches his shirt and pants. I admire my uncle's pencil-thin mustache curving above his upper lip. Someday, I hope to have one like his. We also meet his wife, Thelma, and his two daughters. My cousins are chubby like their dad. They don't look like they get much exercise.

The furnishings in their house are old but well cared-for. "These end tables were my mother's," my uncle tells Dad.

The chairs are covered with clear plastic, which feels sticky against my bare legs. Outside, a creek runs through the yard and into a forest.

"Why don't you kids run outside and play? There's a swing in the back and lots of room to run around," Uncle Lyman's oldest tells us. She's nineteen. His other daughter is two years younger.

They stay inside with my folks.

Once we're outside, where the air seems cooler than in the city, Charles pushes me and says, "These trees remind me of *Little Red Riding Hood*." He runs off, yelling, "The big bad wolf is after us!"

My other brothers join him, running away from me as they scream and race in different directions, playing hide-and-seek. Charles squats low behind some bushes and waits. I'm the wolf, but I pretend I'm a deer with antlers and leap over the creek, following a rabbit trail. I crouch to look for anyone hiding nearby, while I try not to be seen. Dappled light streams through the tree branches onto the greenery and bramble. I make sure to keep our uncle's clapboard house in view.

I love the raw earth smell and enjoy kicking leaves and old branches, but nothing in this place reminds me of San Diego. Although I'm *it*, I haven't found anyone yet. I imagine myself as a grown buck with eight-point antlers, standing among the trees. I guard my brothers, making sure no tigers, lions, or bears interfere with their play.

Mom calls us to come in and say goodbye. As I climb in the car, I discover wrapped gifts for each of us. With Dad's prompting, we sing-song thank yous and settle in for our drive to the next destination. Uncle Lyman and his family stand near our car, first closing the doors for us and then waving as Dad drives away.

Grandma is seated behind Mom and says, "You may open the gifts."

I gasp aloud when I see mine and hold it to my chest. "A baseball shirt!"

All the packages contain beige baseball shirts, each in the correct size and embroidered by Aunt Thelma with a red bird, the Cardinals logo, on the front and the team's name on the back.

Over the car engine's soft hum, Grandma explains, "We'll soon arrive at my brother's. I am looking forward to you boys meeting him."

It's late morning when we approach Great-Uncle Jack's home. We ease onto a curved, asphalt driveway and see a white fence surrounding a green meadow.

James spots horses grazing and exclaims, "Wow, look at those horses!"

"Your Uncle Jack races thoroughbreds," Grandma tells him.

Dad drives through a white gated entrance, turns onto a grassy lane, and pulls up to the two ranch houses. They look just as my cousins described, but they're even better than I could have imagined. The bigger house is a mansion.

An old hickory tree shades a winding path between the two homes. Dad stops the car in front of an old man standing on the walkway. Mom exclaims, "That's Great-Uncle Jack!"

He looks dignified, wearing a black Stetson cowboy hat, red-striped studded shirt, and dark slacks. He leans on a fancy walking stick to steady himself.

Grandma gets out of the car first. "Jack!" she exclaims. "How are you?"

Dad comes to her side and extends his hand. "I'm George. I've been looking forward to meeting you, Great-Uncle Jack."

"Just call me Jack." He returns Dad's handshake. "George, I like your strong grip. So, you're the fella who married my niece?" Mom squeezes between them and wraps her arms around Great-Uncle Jack. They hug for a long time.

"Emma," he says, taking her in. "I ain't seen you in a month of Sundays."

After she releases him, Great-Uncle Jack walks past my brothers and me, all lined up next to the car. He nods to each of us, shakes our hands, and says, "Glad to meetcha." He rubs my head as if it's a crystal ball. My hair is closely cut, and this doesn't bother me. "So, Emma, these are your children?" He points to Charles and says to Mom, "I remember when you were no taller than this boy."

"Let's head out. I know you boys will like the game house." He puts his arm around Grandma and leads the way with the aid of his wooden cane. We walk under the huge hickory tree with lower branches the size of my thighs.

"That tree should be an easy climb," I say to James.

He nods, "Okay, let's climb it before we leave."

Once inside, Great-Uncle Jack puts his hat on one of the pegs by the door. Out his giant front window, everything on the race track seems framed, like a painting in rapid motion. The pounding rhythm of hooves becomes more intense as two horses canter past with their riders. Thundering round the bend, huge clods of dirt fly up like cannon shots as their hooves dig into the track. This ranch is one of the most exciting places I've ever seen.

I ask Mom and Dad, "May I go out there?"

Great-Uncle Jack says, "We will in a short while. I want to show you some things here first." He shifts his cane and rests his forearm on my shoulder. It's uncomfortable, but I keep quiet.

He takes me over to a wall filled with black-and-white photos of himself in various fighting stances. In one picture, he's wearing shiny boxing shorts, dark gloves, and tall, lightweight, black boots. His arms are high, protecting his head. In another, he wears a black T-shirt and flexes his biceps like a bodybuilder. I'd guess he was about twenty in most of these pictures.

Animated, he tells me about them. "After I left the ring, I coached boxing." He punches the air in front of me with the arm not holding the cane. "It was a good living, but I got too old for that. Now I'm into horse racing."

A gold robe drapes his shoulders in the next few pictures; he's huskier and maybe as old as my folks are today. He poses in the winner's circle next to a tan horse with a blue-ribboned wreath around its neck. Great-Uncle Jack's smile is bigger than the jockey's.

"This is Trixie." He points to his palomino. "And this is Dane." He names all the horses. "They all have fancy pedigrees, and they're my loves." His voice trails off. "When their racing and breeding days are over, they live out their lives here. My jockeys and trainers keep them fit by exercising them."

We walk over behind three leather chairs and a couch that face another huge window. Behind us is a full floor-to-ceiling bookcase with a ladder on wheels to reach the books on the top shelves. I climb the ladder and look through gaps in the rows of books, where I can see into the next room.

Behind the counter is a lighted display cabinet full of liquor bottles sparkling like jewels. Across from them are two oak kegs, one on top of the other, with spigots. I climb down the ladder to go into the other room.

There are four tall tables with stools on a polished dance floor. Against a bare, wood-paneled wall stands a jukebox with flashing orange, white, and blue lights that seem to beckon visitors to push its buttons. I press A6 to play "Wake Up, Little Susie" by the Everly Brothers.

"Hey, Gaylloyd!" James shouts at me then races off after Michael, yelling, "*A pool table.*"

It is an impressive table with forest-green felt and dark wood.

James tells Michael, "Let's play. I'll rack 'em up."

"Yeah." Michael rushes to a case on the wall and grabs two pool cues.

* * *

In the early afternoon, my folks and Grandma sit on the couch in front of the big window. With cold drinks in hand, they watch riders on the track. A trainer leans against the fence railing and points to where the track curves, his hands moving as if he is giving instructions to a deaf child. Great-Uncle Jack and I look at a chessboard that is set up, ready for someone to make the first move. I smirk, nod toward my brothers at the pool table, and say, "None of them will play me anymore. I always win."

"Have a seat," my great-uncle directs. "You can have the advantage."

Chess rules designate that white moves first, so I move the king's pawn to center, forward two squares.

"Have you read all those books?" I ask.

"Yeah. Most are about boxing or horses. Do you like to read?"

I watch his move. "My folks bought a whole set of *My Book House.*" I move my bishop. "I've read the first three. They're easier than the rest."

He moves a piece. "Good."

I skip my knight to a forward position as I listen to his advice about money and assets. Then he tells me an anecdote about boxing that makes me laugh and he forwards another pawn. I swap my rook and king and announce, "Castling."

He moves his queen a few squares forward. "Don't put all your eggs in one basket," he cautions.

I want to tell him about my chickens at home that never got a chance to lay eggs, but I don't. I advance my rook's pawn one, not removing my hand from it as I wonder whether I should leave it in that square. I do and nod that it's his turn.

Mom, Dad, and Grandma enter the room and stand over us as Great-Uncle Jack moves.

I move.

He sweeps his queen across the board and captures the pawn in front of my king. "Checkmate."

I slap my forehead. "I didn't see that coming." I look up. My brothers are standing around the table, watching us. "Do you want to play another one?"

He laughs. "That's the spirit, boy."

Phillip asks Mom, "Can we go to the stables and look at the horses?"

"No. We're not staying much longer. Your uncle has lunch for us, and afterward, we must get on our way."

Great-Uncle Jack pats her hand. "Emma, I want to show the boys the track. We won't be long."

She kisses Phillip on the top of his head and says to Great-Uncle Jack, "I was just a kid when I was last here. I stayed the whole week. Think I'll tag along."

Outside, Great-Uncle Jack shows us the barn, the stables, and the jockeys' quarters. Everything is neat and tidy, but up close, the stabled horses are scary. Their teeth are big enough to bite off my hand.

BADMINTON AND AN EAST ST. LOUIS DRIVE

12.

"There's only one right way to hold a badminton racquet," Uncle Arthur explains. "Hold it with the webbing facing the net. And remember, the follow-through is the most important part of the swing."

We've had breakfast, and I'm in the back yard with Uncle Arthur and my brothers. He talked me into this game. Like James and Michael, I'm doing my best to pay attention to his instructions, but I again miss the feathery ball flying at me from the other side of the net.

He reminds us constantly, "Follow-through is the most important thing," and "Keep your eye on the birdie." I imitate his slow-motion swing.

"That's it, Gaylloyd," he says.

The game involves a birdie, which is a strange half sphere crowned with white feathers. It is tossed above the server's head and swatted with a lightweight, oval racquet. The birdie is supposed to fly over the net, a maneuver mastered with practice, or so I'm told.

After completing their chores, our cousins join us to play

doubles. Uncle Arthur explains the rules and designates Paul and Peter as team captains. The better players are paired with the rookies: Peter and James against Paul and me. Everyone else is on the sidelines, awaiting their team's turn.

Paul tosses a coin and shouts, "Tails never fail!" It lands tails. I'm glad I'm on his team. Before we begin, he tells me, "I have a special serving technique."

With his left hand, he tosses the birdie high. He holds his right arm straight, with the racquet flat and facing the net, and swings. The birdie flies over the net. James strikes at the thing, but it lands untouched behind him.

I laugh.

Paul serves again. James tags it, and the birdie flies at my face. I swing upward with all my might, hit it, and watch it fly straight toward the sunny blue sky. Then it turns around and lands ten inches in front of me.

James laughs.

Uncle Arthur reminds us, "Hold the racquet perpendicular to the ground and swing evenly across."

I mentally rehearse the instructions, but I make the same error again.

We rotate in and out of the game with the younger kids in teams against one another. Waiting my turn is the most difficult part. After I play the first round, I watch the other players. With each turn, I get cockier. By match point of the sixth game, I've improved.

James serves a simple lob.

"Oh, this is gonna be easy," I brag aloud, conscious that everyone is watching me.

The birdie seems to hang in the air, but I take my eyes off it, swing, and miss. Feeling stupid, I scream at the birdie and slam my racquet on the ground. It snaps, and only strings keep the broken wood frame together. Everyone stares at me.

Paul yells, "Why did you *do* that? Now we have to buy another one!"

"I'm sorry." Tears well up in my eyes.

"You ruined it for all of us!" Paul glares at me face-to-face. He looks like he wants to take a swing.

I'm humiliated and sorry we can't play any longer. I understand how Humpty Dumpty's friends felt. I wish I could put the racquet back together again.

Uncle Arthur puts his arm around my shoulder. "Gaylloyd, you did well, and everyone had a good time. As important as it is to enjoy yourself, disappointment comes with any game. Controlling your temper is a part of good sportsmanship. For now, I want you to think about why it happened."

Looking at everyone else, he says "All you kids made plenty of mistakes when you were first learning. Don't you remember?"

They all nod.

"Every one of us needs practice. That's the only way to improve." My uncle's wisdom helps ease my pain.

He beckons to the other kids to gather around him and takes car keys from his pocket. "Let's go for a drive. Peter, let your mother know we'll be gone for a short while."

Lettie tugs on my shirt sleeve. "I'll race you to the car," she says and starts to run, with Michael and Phillip close behind.

Her challenge helps me to think about my uncle's advice. I blink back my tears and race to my uncle's black 1955 Mercury. "Shotgun!" I yell and climb in the front by the window.

Sitting behind the steering wheel, Uncle Arthur leans back into his seat. "Uncle Arthur, I'm sorry."

"When I'm unhappy, I take a walk or drive around and think about it. Everything will be fine," he says. "I want to show you around."

"Thanks, Uncle Arthur."

Lettie asks, "Daddy, where are we going?"

"I'm not sure. I thought we'd show the boys our city."

Peter returns and climbs in the back seat next to James. "Dad, I'm ready. Mom says we need to be back for lunch."

Uncle Arthur nods. "Yes son." We tootle down the tree-lined street and leave the neighborhood.

Before long, I notice there are fewer trees and wider sidewalks that are closer to the buildings, leaving no grassy areas between them.

Phillip taps me on the shoulders and says, "This must be the business area."

I try to compare these offices and this part of town with those in downtown San Diego. The concrete streets and sidewalks and the traffic lights are like home, but many buildings here are much older. I can't tell exactly how long they've been around, but it must have been quite a while.

"My Dad has lived here so long, he turns on one street then another, and the next thing you know," Paul whispers loud enough for his dad to hear, "he's lost."

Uncle Arthur laughs and looks into the rearview mirror. "He's right. There are so many ways to get to the same place that at times I forget which way I'm going to get there."

We near a massive church made of huge brown stones the color of dirt. "Can we stop here, Dad?" Peter asks. "This is the Old Catholic Cathedral where we're attending Mass tomorrow. We need to show this church to the guys."

As Uncle Arthur pulls into the parking lot in front of the church entrance, pigeons fly out of the way.

"This is one of the oldest buildings in St. Louis." Paul pauses to think for a moment. "I'm sure it dates far back to the early 1700s, before the Revolutionary War."

"I think it was here even before the Louisiana Purchase," says Peter.

"And we can see the river," Maggie adds. She and Charles giggle. They're almost the same age, and they seem to find everything funny.

Phillip is out of the car first. "This must be the Mississippi River."

I walk across the parking lot and lean over a rock wall above the river bank. A white steamboat makes its' way upriver against the current. A huge red wheel churns on its aft, with several vigorous paddles circling continuously and splashing water. Above is a white sign with bold black lettering that identifies the boat as the *Natchez*.

"That sure is an old boat." I walk to the railing. "It looks just like one of those riverboats Mark Twain wrote about."

Paul, standing near the embankment, looks up at the church's steeple. A copper bell fills the opening at the top. "We go to Mass here every Sunday," he tells me.

Inside the church, sun rays flow through the cathedral's stained-glass windows, highlighting the polished oak pews. In the sun light dust particles dance in random patterns. Tall pillar candles line the aisle to the altar at the far end, and I feel a spiritual ambiance.

I genuflect, touching my right knee to the floor. Then I go into the pew, kneel and face the communion table at the front. With my hands folded, eyes closed, and head bowed, I pray for forgiveness for breaking the badminton racquet.

I can't imagine not being a Catholic. The parochial school I've always attended makes me feel secure. I take for granted that what I learn there prepares me for what my folks already know about life.

I'm the last one out of the church. When I climb back into the car, no one is in my place up front.

Uncle Arthur pulls out of the parking lot. "Next," he says, "we'll cross the bridge over the Mississippi River."

On the other side, I can tell we're in a different city. Most of the houses here look as if no one cares for them. Many were painted so long ago, they're faded now. Debris scatters on the sidewalks and along the gutters.

"This is East St. Louis," Uncle Arthur explains. "We're in a different city and a different state."

"What state?" James asks.

"Illinois," Lettie says.

Everything appears dirty. There are rusted vehicles double-parked in front of rows of apartment buildings, many with tires that seem to have been flat for years. People walk around the cars to continue on the sidewalk.

Compared to our house in San Diego or Uncle Arthur's house or even the one we stayed at in El Reno, Oklahoma, this neighborhood makes me feel ashamed for the people living here.

I'm happy I don't have to stay.

Paul tells me, "We have relatives on this side of the river, but we never visit them."

Uncle Arthur stiffens. "And remember, we don't talk about them!"

Paul looks out the window. I have no idea why they wouldn't visit a blood relative. We have no kinfolk in San Diego, but if we did, we'd see them all the time.

We wind through one community and then another. Some look like the ones we drove through when we first entered East St. Louis, and some are much cleaner.

I expect my uncle to admit he's not sure he knows where we are, but the topic never comes up. "Is he lost?" I ask Lettie.

"He'd never admit it if he was," she says. "I'm anxious to get home for lunch."

"Yeah, me, too. I like where you live."

EAST ST. LOUIS REVISITED
13.

With James close behind me, I push the door open. It slams against the inside wall.

"Slow down boys," Aunt Ruth tells us. "If you're looking for your folks, they're in the other room." She nods toward the kitchen door that opens to the hall.

Mom sits on the couch across from the piano and talks to Dad. I hurry over and James catches up.

Mom, with Dad's hands in hers, says, "Honey, after being out all morning with Ruth and Grandma, I just don't feel up to going out again now. Ruth's getting lunch for the kids. After I rest, I'll get things ready for tomorrow's game."

I begin my blow-by-blow account of the morning, but I don't mention breaking the racquet. "We went to East St. Louis. Uncle Arthur drove us all over the place."

"Son, that's great, but you interrupted our conversation."

"Sorry, Dad." I'm embarrassed.

James squeezes between Dad and Mom on the couch. Dad pats the top of James's thigh. I'm disappointed he doesn't seem to care much about what I saw in East St. Louis.

Taking Mom's hands in his, he says, "Emma, I can understand your being tired. Now that the boys are back, we can visit Sarah. Not sure how long we'll be there."

Mom places her cupped hands on her stomach. "I'd love to meet her, but…"

"Sweetheart, Sarah's getting on in years. What with tomorrow's game being an all-day event, today is our last chance to see my stepmother."

Mom says, "George, you'll just have to visit her without me."

He releases her hands. "Okay then, stay and rest. Ruth and Mother will take care of you."

"I'm glad you understand. Please give her my best."

"Gaylloyd, you're coming with me to meet my stepmother." Dad seems disappointed.

James says, "Mom! I want to go with Daddy. Daddy, can I go?"

"You *may*." Dad helps James scoot from the couch. "Go eat, both of you. We'll leave when you're finished."

James leans on Dad, kisses him on the cheek, and then runs to the kitchen.

"Tomato soup and BLT sandwiches," Aunt Ruth says as we walk in. She's at the stove, and my brothers are already seated around the table with Peter and our younger cousins. Paul spreads mayonnaise on the bread, and Lettie stands next to him, slicing tomatoes.

Michael asks, "What's a BLT?"

I have the same question, as the bacon aroma commands my attention. Taking a seat, I look at him knowing he's likely to turn his nose up at any unfamiliar food.

Lettie says, "It's a sandwich on toasted bread with mayonnaise, slices of bacon—that's what B stands for. Lettuce is the L, and tomatoes are the T."

"It sounds delicious," I say. "Need help, Aunt Ruth?"

"No, thanks. I have all the help I need. Lunch will be ready in a minute."

"We have to hurry. Dad's taking us to meet his stepmother."

Aunt Ruth hands to me a bowl of soup. "You start."

I lift the bowl to my mouth. I love the rich, smooth tomato taste, and nearly empty it in one gulp.

Aunt Ruth says, "Gaylloyd, slow down. Use your soup spoon. Your dad won't leave without you."

* * *

Mom waves from the front door as we climb into the car to leave.

As Dad drives away, he says, "I met my stepmother when I moved to St. Louis to finish high school. Years earlier, she and your granddad left Mississippi together to find work."

Dad has told me about her. Now, I'm about to meet her. "Is she your mother?"

"No, she's *not* my mother. My mother died right after my sister was born. I was four. Sissy was a week old when Sarah and Dad left us with Aunt Myra." He draws out every word. "Your granddad told Aunt Myra he'd send for us when he found a place to live. So, we stayed with Aunt Myra, waiting. And in all those years," Dad adds, his hands tightening on the steering wheel, "he only sent her four dollars!"

He's quiet as we cross the bridge into East St. Louis, then he glances at me and asks, "How was Aunt Myra supposed to buy what Sissy and I needed on four dollars?"

As we drive past stores and other buildings, I watch for anything I might recognize from our earlier drive with Uncle Arthur, but we're in a different part of town.

Dad looks around and comments about things in the area. He continues in a talkative mood. "I loved growing up with Aunt Myra," he tells us. "I don't remember my own mother, so Myra is the only mother I've known. She was strict, though, and she rarely said she loved me. We were competitive, especially picking cotton. I worked hard, but she'd always outdo Sissy and me. The more we picked, the more money we made."

Dad tells us one story after another about living with Aunt Myra. "Her husband once whipped me for not working fast enough. Aunt Myra broke a broom handle over the man's back and dared him to show his face on her property again.

"I was nineteen when I left home. I jumped a freight car to find my dad and stayed with him and Sarah to go to high school. Where I grew up, there were no high schools for colored students.

"You boys don't know how much better your lives are than mine was. Unlike my own father, who abandoned me, I'll always be by your side."

Another story, which I've heard many times, is about the difficulties of living with his dad while going to school in St. Louis. Mom says he repeats his stories because he feels his father deserted him.

"My dad had a trucking business. It was during the Depression when I arrived to live with him. Once, I invited some classmates to study at the house. I wanted my dad to meet my friends. When he came home, he yelled at us, 'Turn off my lights. Get your hands out of my pocket!' My friends left. I never invited anyone over again. But Sarah was always kind to me."

Dad's anecdotes gave me better insight into his struggles growing up.

"Is this where you lived with your dad and Sarah?" I ask.

"Yes, it is. See what I mean by your lives being better than mine?"

I nod and say, "Yes, Dad."

He veers off the congested street into an area Uncle Arthur had avoided. People living around here seem not to care for flowers or other plants. Lining the street are parades of gnarly oak trees. Cars are parked haphazardly along the street. Next to building entrances are debris-filled cans, with much of the trash scattered on the grassless ground. I'm disappointed Sarah lives in such an ugly place.

"Your granddad died five years ago. Sarah has lived alone ever since."

"Oh, here we are." Dad sounds surprised that we've arrived.

The street has several identical buildings with littered walkways separating their towering faded beige walls. They all have rectangular windows spaced evenly at each of the six levels.

He finds a place to park. I open the car door and wait for Dad to lock up.

"I lived a few blocks from here with Sarah and your granddad while finishing high school," he says as he guides us to the entrance of a building. "I left here after I graduated and joined the Navy. Let's see," he stops walking. "I was twenty-two."

We climb the stairs to the second floor and knock on an apartment door.

"Come on in," a frail voice calls.

Dad turns the knob and walks in. I follow him, trailed by James.

An older woman, propped up with cushions, fills her twin bed in her one-room apartment. A table with a hotplate on it sits against the wall near two wooden chairs. A sofa is pushed against the far wall next to a large, faded refrigerator with a rusty door.

The walls and window shades are brown and look like they're streaked from years of cigarette smoke.

Rays of the late-afternoon sun fight their way through the stains from one of the windows onto an aluminum wash tub sitting on a table. A few unwashed dishes poke above its rim.

"You come right on in." the woman beckons us from her bed against the wall at the far end of the room across from the kitchen. Above her headboard is the only other window in the room, but a manila shade blocks the view. Make yourselves at home." The small sofa has soiled arms with stuffing, discolored with old smoke stains peeking from random rips. A banged-up coffee can sits on the floor next to her bed. Her hair hangs to her shoulders. I'm not accustomed to the cooked Vaseline smell in her hair. Her dry ashy skin is a rust color. She needs to use the bottle of Jergen's lotion lying on a table near her bed.

Four pillows surround her heavy body, and two more are at her back. All she has on is a flimsy, see-through, pink nightgown. A thick pink blanket covers her lap. When I see her flat breasts, I jerk my head away.

"Sarah," Dad says, "I know we just got here, but where's the head?"

"Down the hallway, George. Everyone here on the second floo' shares it, so you might have ta' wait a bit."

When Dad leaves us standing in the middle of the room

without making introductions, I feel abandoned.

She waves her hand toward the couch and chairs. "I'm Sarah. Sit over there." James takes her up on the suggestion. I keep standing.

"I hope you don't mind me not gettin' up," she apologizes. "I am feelin' poorly today. It's so good to see you children."

"Yes, ma'am," I say, and nod.

When Dad returns, I sit on a wooden chair. Talking to Dad, Sarah's excited hand dances with her words and low-pitched voice. The loose skin on her arms emphasizes her lack of strength as it waves to and fro in rhythm with her slow drawl. Even with her smile I feel uncomfortable being in the room with her. "Thank God your daddy left me some money," she says to Dad.

"I'll send something to help."

"Oh, no. I have enough. I use it to pay the rent and buy myself some food." She looks from him to me. "I gits around to visit a few of my friends now and then. No, no, don't worry your head over me, honey. I'm doing well."

"*Pssst,*" I whisper to James and nod at a copper bowl with a wide rim on the floor, next to her bed. "See that? It's a spittoon." Besides smoking, she chews tobacco. My stomach curdles.

James snickers and covers his mouth. "Looks like she's missed it a few times."

As Dad tells Sarah about Mom, she leans over the bowl and spits. It lands near her target. The sight disgusts me, yet I instantly feel guilty about feeling that way.

"May James and I go outside?"

Sarah winks at Dad. "Sho'nuff. I know you youngsters don't wanna hear no old folks talk."

Dad laughs. "Stay on the steps," he says. "I'll be down in two shakes of a dead lamb's tail." He says that when he wants us to wait for him.

Outside, James whispers, "I'm glad you got us out." He jumps two steps at a time down to the main floor. We sit on the landing above the front steps.

I say, "Watching Sarah reminds me of a story I read. I don't remember the title, but it describes three kids sitting on grass outside a courthouse somewhere in Mississippi, watching the local alcoholic. He sits against an old magnolia tree and sips from a Coke bottle wrapped in a brown paper bag. After a while, he sets the bottle down next to him and dozes off.

"One of the boys says to his friends, 'I bet that bottle has whiskey.' He crawls over to the man, lifts the bottle, and gulps a huge swig. His friends laugh as he gags and spits out a brown blob of juice.

"'That whiskey must be strong, or he's not used to drinking that stuff,' one of them guffaws. Dropping the bottle, the boy grabs his stomach and falls to the ground. He rolls onto his side and spews out what's left in his mouth.

"All the commotion wakes the drunk. He leans to his side, exposing a can of Skoal underneath him. 'Boy, that stuff ain't whiskey,' he crows. 'It's chawin' tobacco spit.'"

James busts a gut and slides between the rails off the landing. The fall doesn't stop his chortling. He dusts himself off and runs back to where I'm bent over laughing. "It's chawin' tobacco spit!" he says over and over, grabbing his stomach and rolling on the porch to imitate the boy in the story. Even though the sun is still high in the sky, the street lights are on. They're spaced quite a few yards apart along the sidewalks and will spotlight passersby later in the evening. A family with three small children walks past us into Sarah's building.

"Hello," they say one at a time as they pass.

A kid about our age comes out of the building and sits with us. "I live upstairs," he says.

"We're visiting my dad's stepmother," I say and give him her name.

"Oh, Miss Sissin," he says.

"No, it's pronounced Sissón. Think of it this way. When girls at home chase me, they scream *kiss on sis-són*." I laugh.

James says, "Ha, you wish!" He tells the boy, "We got here this week. We've already met our mom's relatives." He describes Uncle Jack's two houses, his patio, and the horse track.

"Yeah," the boy says.

"Uh-huh," James says. "And our cousins live in one of the richest areas of St. Louis," declaring that the street at Uncle Arthur's house is much cleaner than the one in front of this building.

"We're from San Diego," I say. "Mañana we're going to the Cardinals' game. They're a lot better than the Padres back home, even though I like our home team."

"Y'all sure talk funny," he interrupts our bragathon.

"What do you mean?"

"Well, here you is, a sittin' on this here porch and all, and you talkin' about that there patio."

"Yeah, so?" I say.

"Oh, at home we call porches patios," James tells him.

"Okay, then, what's *mañana*?"

I tell him we live in a neighborhood where lots of people speak Spanish. "It's the way we say tomorrow at home." This is the first time I realize I mix Spanish and English.

Dad's footsteps echo on the stairs. "Hello! Are you ready?"

"Yes siree!" I leap to my feet.

"Adiós." I wave to the kid, who's still sitting on the landing.

Dad says nothing but wipes away a tear as we drive away.

THE BASEBALL GAME

14.

"Wake up! Wake up!" Paul shouts.

As anxious as I am for the day to begin, I play possum, pretending to be asleep, a game I play at home when Dad tries to get me up. Anyway, we're not leaving for another four hours.

Paul jumps feet-first on the bed, shouting, "*Gaylloyd!* We're going to the baseball game today with Grandma!" He almost lands on me.

I shove him onto the floor. "Get off me." He pulls the covers with him as he falls between the beds. I grab them back.

"Hey, that hurts," he gripes as he jerks the bedspread and tears it.

Grandma's voice from the kitchen is just what I need to hear. "I won't miss this game for all the world. I am going to watch my Cardinals play if it kills me. They'll always be my team, win or lose."

I don't know who she's talking to, but I'd guess it's my dad. He's not a big sports fan, because he's usually out to sea during baseball season. I've never been to a ballgame with him.

Dad calls my name like it's two words. "Gay-Lloyd, up and at 'em!"

I jump up and rush to the top of the staircase. "Who told him

I'm not out of bed yet?"

Peter shrugs as he passes me in the hall.

I holler to Dad, "I can't get into the bathroom yet! The other kids are in there. I have to wait my turn."

"There's another." Peter points to the door he's come from.

"I thought it was your parents'."

"You can use it. Or just take your stuff to the one downstairs," he says, clinging to his toothbrush and a towel wrapped around his waist.

Once I finish washing and dressing, I breathe in the bacon aroma and head to the stairs.

Mom's voice wafts up from the kitchen. "Maple syrup and waffles!"

After breakfast, my cousins and brothers, all wearing our embroidered Cardinals shirts, run up and down the stairs to get whatever we need during the game.

From her room upstairs, Lettie yells, "*Mary*! Help Maggie get dressed."

"Stop your horseplay," Aunt Ruth says, chiding Michael, Phillip, and Maggie. "Are all of you ready?"

"Uncle Lyman and his whole family will join us at the stadium," Grandma says.

I'm not used to being around so many females, and their chatter exhilarates me. I pound my fist into a baseball glove Paul loaned me.

"James, come here, and bring Mark's shoes with you," Mom hollers. He runs past me to get the shoes from his luggage, almost knocking me down. Just as I get to the top of the stairs, Dad calls me. I slide down the railing to the bottom.

"We don't slide down the railing in this house," Aunt Ruth scolds.

"Boy, what's gotten into you?" Dad turns to Aunt Ruth and adds apologetically, "We don't do that at home, either! Gaylloyd, take your brothers out to the car. We're ready to go."

My cousins are just as packed in their car as we are in ours, but they appear calmer than we do. I sit in the back, trying to get settled, with my brothers bouncing on the seat. I roll down my window and wait for Mom and Dad.

Seeing Grandma approach our car, Phillip shouts, "Grandma's riding with us!"

"Yay!" my brothers yell and don't quiet down until she's seated next to me in the back. She smiles at Mark as she pulls him onto her lap.

Mom's sister, Aunt Evelyn, took us to see the San Diego Padres when she visited us from Los Angeles, but the radio is the closest I've ever been to the famous Busch Stadium here in St. Louis. Today, I couldn't be more eager to see it firsthand.

During Grandma's last visit to San Diego, she and I listened to every Cardinals game on the radio. She shouted pitching instructions to Larry Jackson and gave "atta boys" to the rest of the team. Her favorites are Stan Musial, Joe Cunningham, and Wally Moon. They're like old friends. I'm convinced she personally knows every one of them.

Grandma, looking around me and back to the house, says, "What's taking your dad so long?" She fidgets with her white lace handkerchief, but I think she's trying to be patient. I admire her dark-blue dress with tiny white flower print, her gold-rimmed glasses, and polished black granny shoes.

Aunt Ruth, Uncle Arthur, Mom, and Dad come from the house as if in answer to Grandma's question. In both cars, we kids cheer.

It's about ten o'clock, and the morning is muggy. Grandma sings a baseball song about Willie Mays, "Say Hey." I listen for a while until James interrupts her, pretending he's a broadcaster, and calls imaginary pitches, swings, and strikes.

Michael punches Phillip on the shoulder. Charles laughs. He's next to them, and all three are on their knees, waving at our cousins following our car.

"Sit down," Mom tells my brothers.

Uncle Lyman and his family arrive at the stadium before we do. Uncle Clyde's wife, Aunt Donie, stands with them in front of the ticket window, and I figure the guy with her must be Uncle Clyde. Uncle Gus and his adopted son, Benj, are talking to Uncle Lyman.

A bunch of tickets in hand, Uncle Gus waves to us. "Okay, we're all here," he says and hands a fistful of tickets to Mom. "We're sitting together."

Grandma asks, "Where's the seating?"

Uncle Gus tells her, "Over the Cardinals' bullpen."

"Grandma, those are great seats!" says Paul.

She beams.

"I brought cushions," Uncle Lyman says, handing one to each one of us.

Inside the stadium, I sit next to Grandma. She lays the roster open on my lap. "Look at this. Larry Jackson is starting."

"Yeah, number twenty," I say.

"Uh-huh. He has a heck of a slider."

The loudspeaker blares, "*And here comes the lineup.*" A voice full of static introduces the players to the frenzied cheers from the crowd.

Joe Cunningham walks right in front of me onto the field. I can't believe my eyes. My jaw drops. I know him from the radio and have his card in my collection.

"Gaylloyd, stop gawking," Mom says, tugging my shoulders downward. I didn't realize I was standing, blocking her view. I sit.

The audience sings the national anthem with the announcer and cheers when he finishes. The home team is on the field.

* * *

At the bottom of the second inning, there's only one out.

"Wally's up," Grandma says, as her hero leaves the dugout. Her hands cupped, megaphone-like, she shouts, "*Wally, you've never let me down!*"

He looks up, smiles, and winks at her. She glows, dabbing her eyes with a hankie.

It's the first pitch to him. Wally takes it. A hit. The ball bounces past third. The fielder slings it to first. Wally slides to the base, feet first. "Safe!"

Grandma turns to Arthur, "I can always count on him."

The next two hits are fly-outs with Wally still on base.

"Hot dogs—popcorn—ice-cream—Cracker Jacks! Hot dogs—popcorn...!" yells the burly hawker. He waves a candy bar in the air as he makes his way down the aisle toward us.

"Hot dog right here," says Dad.

The vendor comes over to us.

"George," Mom says, "I want an ice cream." The rest of us call out our choices.

In the middle of the fifth, Stan Musial's at bat, with two hits on the board, two outs, and runners on third and second. He has three balls and one strike against him.

"It's a swing and a miss. Strike two," the metallic loudspeaker thunders. "Full count."

Grandma nudges me in the ribs. "Watch closely now."

The pitcher takes a red bandanna from his back pocket, wipes his forehead, stuffs the cloth back, and scowls at the batter. He pauses for a split-second and leans forward, both hands behind his back. In one motion, he raises his arms, lifts his left leg, and hurls the hardball to the plate.

The bat connects. *Crack!*

The white sphere flies high toward center field. I lose sight of it. The crowd rises to its feet in unison and goes berserk.

"It's a home run!" screams the broadcaster.

Uncle Gus's son, Benj, on Grandma's right, jumps to his feet with the crowd.

Grandma rises off her seat, arms flailing, knocking Benj backward. His dad catches him, keeping him from hitting his head on the bench.

She turns, looking at him as if seeing him for the first time, and says, "I'm sorry, boy," and then pulls him back to his seat. "He seems okay," Grandma says to my uncle. "No blood." She turns back to the game. I smile.

Uncle Gus pats his boy's head. "Son, are you all right?"

His answer is drowned out by the cheering crowd. James and Lettie shout and jump up and down.

James screams, "We're gonna win! I just know it."

Benj pumps his arms in the air and hugs Lettie, rocking side to side. I look at Grandma, expecting her to snarl, but her look is enough. Benj lets Lettie go and leans into Aunt Ida Mae's arms.

After nine innings, the Cardinals win, five to three. The day is hot, my clothes are sticky, but I'm ecstatic at our big win.

The crowd grabs its stuff, leaving hot dog wrappers, soda pop cans, beer cups, and other rubbish. As I rush down the aisle, I crunch the peanut shells I dropped . Everyone's jovial as we head home.

In the parking lot on our way to the car, Dad says, "Gaylloyd, we're coming back here tomorrow. I want to teach you some of the basics of driving."

I think to myself, wait 'til my friends find out my dad taught me how to drive while I was here!

THE DRIVING LESSON

15.

After lunch the following day, Dad and I go back to the Busch Stadium parking lot, which now serves as my driving classroom. He parks under one of the light poles.

Pointing to the dashboard panel, he says, "Son, these letters are important. The D is drive, R is reverse, and P is park. The dial here is the speedometer. It tells how fast the car is going. On the floor by my feet are two pedals."

I look down at his feet.

"The left one's the brake and the other one is the accelerator." As he explains these mechanisms and describes other aspects of the Packard, I listen and watch. When he finishes explaining, he pulls away and drives past rows of empty parking spaces. He demonstrates and repeats many driving points, such as checking the mirrors.

He stops next to an empty ticket booth near one of the stadium entrances. "Now, let's see how well you do."

My emotions change from joy to fear and then high anxiety. Before we change positions, he puts the key into my sweaty hand, which feels like being initiated into manhood. Once I'm behind the steering wheel, I insert the key in the ignition, turn it to the right, and hear a loud grinding noise.

"Let go of the key!" he shouts.

I do, and the engine hums.

We sit and listen. Dad takes a deep breath, looks out the window and then at me before he says, "Now put it in drive, and softly push the accelerator."

I gradually press the gas pedal, and the engine's sound increases until it roars like a dozen fierce lions, but there's no movement.

"Ease up on the pedal," Dad points to the emergency brake and smiles. "Release the emergency brake."

I don't want to make another mistake, so I turn the car off. I feel nervous and stupid. I look at his face to see if he's frustrated or upset. He's not frowning, but I'm sure he's not pleased.

"Turn the car on gently. Once the engine is running, release the emergency brake, and ease your foot down on the gas."

I turn the key and quickly release it.

"That's much better," he says.

The engine hums and sounds good. "Dad, I feel ready."

"Okay, now put your foot on the brake and release the emergency brake."

My foot feels the brakes take hold.

"Move the gear shift to the drive position like I showed you."

I step on the accelerator and take my foot off the brake pedal so fast that the car lurches. I slam my foot down on the brake and almost jettison Dad through the windshield. His head hits the dash.

"Remember what I told you—the car has a sensitive touch." He rubs his temples with the tips of his fingers. "Maybe this isn't such a good idea."

"One more chance, Dad, please. I'll do better. I promise."

"All right, Gaylloyd." He sighs. "Easy does it."

I carefully press the gas pedal with a light touch. We inch forward, taking a full minute to drive from one light pole to the next.

"Son, you can go faster."

"Okay." I accelerate and learn to keep going and not stop at each aisle.

On television car chases, the driver rocks the steering wheel to and fro, so I do it to impress Dad with what I know. The car swerves right, then left, then right again.

"Gaylloyd! Stop right here!"

I stop in the middle of an aisle. "Before you go any farther, I need to explain that, most of the time, you want to go straight, so follow the aisles. Turn the wheel only to guide the car."

After several attempts, I learn how to make a smooth turn without jerking and abrupt braking. I don't rock the steering wheel. I drive straight and pay attention to the parking lot layout. Dad has me practice U-turns and backing up while looking over my shoulder.

After about an hour of practice and his coaching, my driving improves. "When you come to the pole with the green and white sign, make a left turn."

I turn at the appropriate corner and grin at him.

His huge smile tells me I'm doing everything well.

I park. "How did I do?"

He cracks a grin. "You did real good. We'll save the parallel parking for another day. You've learned the basics." He reaches over to rub my head.

I dodge his hand. "Aw, Dad!"

He takes back the driver's seat as I scoot to the passenger side. "You'll do all right. We'll do this again in Winona."

"Dad," I say, "you're the greatest.

A DIFFERENT WORLD
16.

We listen to the radio for the four-hour ride to Memphis. As Dad drives into town, Elvis Presley is introduced by the deejay, who says to him, *"Elvis, I read in the newspaper about negro clubs y'all been at. Now tell me this. Do you have a lot of them folks for fans?"*

Elvis clears his throat. *"The only thing Niggers can do for me is buy my records and shine my shoes."*

Dad snaps the radio off, leaving only the sound of air passing through open windows.

"Mom, what did he say?" I ask.

"I can't believe what he said," she tells Dad.

He pushes a button on the radio. "I'll find another station."

The broadcaster of the new station is lively and funny. By the sound of his voice, I'm sure he's a negro.

"We're almost there," Dad says. "Look for the house number. It's somewhere along this street."

"Dad, I see the number," I say. "It's that one." I point to a light-brown house with an ornate black metal rail around a covered porch, where four people are standing.

He parallel parks the car. His cousins, Bubba and Shirley, meet us at our car. Bubba towers over his wife but isn't as tall as Dad. Their two children crowd in front of them. The boy is my height and about my age. He pats his sister's shoulder and says, "I'm Lee, and this ma sista, Candy."

She smiles, "Glad to meet y'all."

Shirley wraps her graceful, dark-brown arms around Mom. "It's so wonderful y'all's come."

As we enter the house, Shirley calls out our names, though she doesn't seem to know who is who.

"Can I show Graceland to Gaylloyd?" Lee asks his mom.

"Not now. Take him later. Show your cousin where to put his luggage in your room, then wash up. We're eating supper."

After dinner, Lee and I rush out the door before we're asked to help wash the dishes.

He introduces me—his cousin from California—to friends and neighbors we meet on the way. The farther we walk from Lee's house, the more different the neighborhood feels. White picket fences around some of the houses break up the ubiquitous look of manicured lawns. Flowers brighten the pathways. Lee doesn't seem to know anyone around here and walks past people without even saying hello.

Lee's walk is quick, his attitude determined. I feel hurried as I follow him eight blocks to a tall brick wall beside towering trees. A copper plate embedded in the wall welcomes *invited* guests inside Elvis's mansion. There is a locked, double-hinged, iron gate across the driveway entrance.

Lee stops there. "This is Graceland," he says. "We cain't go in, but we can look. It's nice. What do you think? Like it?"

"It's all right." Like a bee sting, the radio interview I heard earlier still smarts. I refuse to admit I'm impressed. "It's a nice-looking house."

"House?" He turns from admiring the place. "It ain't a house. It's a mansion!"

"Yeah." I stand behind him and look over his shoulders. "C'mon. Let's go."

I walk back along the same street we came, and he catches up. He's quiet again, so I talk. "I miss home. I swim almost every day at the navy base near our house. I really like my Catholic school, St.

Jude's Academy. We have the best track and field team in the district." I look over at him. He's glances back at the mansion.

"I bet you're on your school's track team, right?" I ask.

"Me? No." Still looking behind us, he asks, "Can you run?"

I snicker. "Can I run? I ran the hundred-yard dash in eleven seconds and came in first!"

"Well, that's good, 'cause you're going to need to run fast now."

I laugh. "What for?"

"Look behind you."

Two blocks away, six boys bear down on us. I can't make out what they're yelling. I momentarily freeze and stare at them. When I turn to ask Lee what's going on, he's so far ahead of me, I barely hear him as he shouts, "*Run, you fool! Run!*"

One of the guys gets near enough for me to see a metal pipe in his hand. I take off again, but the guy manages to pull at my shirt. I'm lucky he can't hold onto it, but he almost breaks his neck, trying to grab me. I run in a wild zigzag pattern like a hare, then I jump a white picket fence, run through the back yard, and leap over the fence on the other side. Lee is nowhere to be seen. I glance back. Two more guys have caught up with the first. One has a knife, one has a broken bottle, and all three are already over the fence.

I round a corner and see Lee several blocks ahead of me. I sprint as he turns off a street between houses like his. I look behind me to see if I'm outrunning these bullies, but one of them is hot on my tail. The sunlight glints off his knife blade.

The white bully yells, "Nigger!"

Out of breath and with my heart pounding out of my chest, I take the same turn Lee took. I hear the loud thud and muffled grunt of someone falling behind me but don't look back, as I hightail it through an unfenced yard and onto another street. There, I see Lee up farther ahead, waiting alongside three friends. I slow, and as I get nearer, I zigzag and sing out, "*Meep-meep,*" the roadrunner's sounds.

Lee is bent over, panting. He looks up at me with anger distorting his face. "They don't like us coming into their neighborhood."

A burly friend of his hits his palm with a baseball bat. "And we don't want them in ours. Only negros live here. White folks don't come around. We don't get along."

I look at a house across the street where small children are playing a game, perhaps hide-n-seek. I say, "Negroes aren't the only ones who live in my neighborhood. Many of my friends are Filipinos and Mexicans, and they live on my street."

"What are Filipinos?" Lee's friend asks.

I'm surprised by his question and stop for a moment to think. "Oh, they're people like us. Well, not exactly like us. Rodney's Filipino. Marco is Mexican and has straight hair like Rodney's, but he's darker. Bobby is Irish or white, I guess."

Lee asks, "You guess? Is he Irish or white?"

I shrug, not sure what to say. "My friends aren't all the same color. It's never been important to us. Bobby said he's Irish. Maybe all white people are Irish."

Three girls not much older than I am pass us, going the other way as they talk and laugh. I stop to watch them for a moment.

"Sports and girls, that's what we talk about. As far as girls go, I'm full of gab but no action." I stand up straight. "Girls like me all the same."

Once we get to Lee's house, we climb the stairs and stand at the railing, looking up at the cloudless, dark sky.

"Man," says Lee, "you live some kinda life that just ain't real."

WINONA, MISSISSIPPI
17.

We eat lunch before we leave Bubba and Shirley's house. Once we have been on the road for about two hours, we pass a highway sign thanking visitors who are leaving Tennessee. Next to it is another welcoming our arrival into another state.

Drawing out each syllable as if they are tantalizing morsels to chew on, Dad says, "This is the state of Mis-sis-sip-pi." His smile reaches both ears. "I'm almost home."

Phillip is up front with him. With his right hand, Dad taps his knee as if running his fingers up and down piano keys.

Sweltering air from the open window blows in my face as I watch the Mississippi scenery roll by. From horizon to horizon, trees tower over dense bushes. Even though the land is flat, I can't see any houses in the distance or birds in the sky.

Dad motions to the passing woods and his face lights up. "When I was a kid, my friends and I hunted squirrels and opossums in places like this. There's nothing like roasting opossum and serving pieces over gravy with cornbread, collard greens, and sweet potatoes."

I haven't ever seen an opossum and have no idea what one really looks like. "What's it like to hunt them? Did you have a rifle?"

"No, we used snares. We tied a thick string between branches in a bush to lay the traps. Once, we shook an opossum out of a tree into a net. Boy, that was *scary*. We put the net and all in a wooden box, closed the lid, and listened to it growl all the way back home. Aunt Myra used a gun to its head."

"What's that old saying, George?" Mom smiles at him, then at my brothers and me. "You can take a boy out of the country, but you can't take the country out of a boy."

In his deepest Southern accent, Dad teases his reply. "Aw, shucks, ma'am, I's just telling th' boy a li'l story. Ain't no harm in that, I reckon."

I like hearing Dad's stories. From the beginning of our trip, he's talked so much about Aunt Myra, I can't hardly wait to meet her. I have no idea what Winona will be like.

As we drive through town, people sit in front of stores, fanning themselves and watching our car go by. Our car looks newer and cleaner than any of the other cars.

"I bet these people have never seen a new car like ours," James says.

The dirt road and open lands tell me we're out of town before Dad announces, "Well, that was downtown."

It's early July, so cornfields nearly as tall as I am line both sides of the road. Everything between us and the end of the Earth is covered by green and gold tassels of corn stalks. "We're getting closer to Aunt Myra's house," Dad says, and my anticipation blossoms.

"Are we there yet?" Michael asks as he bounces next to me.

"Almost," Mom says.

Michael looks at me cross-eyed. I rub his head, and he pulls away.

"Will we see cotton?" Phillip asks.

Dad takes a deep breath but doesn't answer. He has told us quite a few stories about picking cotton when he was a kid, but now he seems distracted. He stares through the windshield at the road, studying everything we pass.

On the driver's side, the cornfields give way to lush greenery. Small groups of black birds glide over a ditch alongside the road, where sunlight reflects off the water. As Dad slows the car, dust continues to rise behind us. There are houses and leafy trees ahead. We stop chattering.

"It won't be long now," he announces.

There are very few people out in their front yards. The houses here have simple roofs, wide front porches, and are sided with wooden planks in various shades of whitewash. The arching branches of honey locusts, black walnuts, and persimmon trees shade the road. As Dad slows the car to a creep, the dust behind us settles down.

Across from the houses is a meadow with grass as high as the car, and behind it, a gray barn, a squat building, and a big, white house. "That's it," Mom says.

Dad drives in through a gate and parks in the shade of a sprawling catalpa tree that has one heavy limb nearly touching the ground. "We're here." He sighs in relief.

I open my door and jump out, stretching my arms above my head, fingers clasped and back arched, relieved to be out in the midday sun. I breathe in the sweet smell of as many of the white catalpa flowers as will fit in my hands. An old tire, suspended by a rope from one of its thick limbs, spins in the warm breeze.

Mom looks at Dad and laughs. He puts his arm around her and pulls her close. "Thank the Lord we got here in one piece," she says. Arm in arm, they turn to look at the house.

A tall, lean woman bursts out of the front door. "Oh, my word," she cries, as she hurries down the porch steps and embraces Dad. They rock side to side. "I looks up and there y'all is, a-standin' here. Emma, it's so good to see y'all." She hugs Mom. "I thought y'all would never get here."

They prattle on and on about the drive from Memphis until Charles asks, "Daddy, who's this lady?"

Dad lifts him and settles him in his arms. "Son, this is your Aunt Myra."

"Hello, Aunt Myra," we all say in one exuberant voice.

"And this must be Gaylloyd." She grabs me by the shoulders. "Boy, I ain't seen you since you was just a baby. Let me take a good look at you. I woulda never knowed y'all if you hadn't a come with your daddy. I remember, when I changed your diaper, you had yellow mushy poo all over your small behind."

My face flushes.

"You and your mama was on your way to California when y'all was last here. You were nothin' but a year." She turns to Mom. "And you were pregnant. Which one's that, Emma?"

"This is James. He's my second child." Mom introduces each one of us.

"Come in, come in," Aunt Myra says. "Y'all can't be standing out here all day long." We go up to the house. "Goodness gracious, I didn't know if y'all a-comin' today or tomorrow, so I got all gussied up this morning, just in case."

Her pale-blue cotton dress, trimmed with a light-yellow ribbon, compliments her jet-black hair, which is parted in the middle, braided, and arranged in two loops on the back of her head. Her face and Dad have similar wide cheekbones and strong jawlines. He says this reflects their East African Hadzabe ancestors and Mississippi Choctaw heritage.

Before we reach the stairs, she stops then leads us toward the masonry block building next door. "Before y'all take your things inside, I'll show you around." She takes Charles's hand in her bony fingers and walks a few yards away from her house. "This here is my store. I built it not long after the last time you been here. I run it myself, George." She smiles at Dad.

The store is a simple rectangular building with several small windows above my head. A bell rings when I open the green wooden screen door that slams shut behind us. The sparse inventory includes brands I recognize from home: Betty Crocker all-purpose flour, Morton salt, Crisco shortening, Brer Rabbit molasses, and C & H pure cane sugar. Open fifty-pound burlap bags stand upright near the cash register, full of black-eyed peas, rice, and barley. Aunt Myra pats me on the shoulder and points to them, with their scoops inside buried up to the handles. "Customers can weigh their purchases on the scale here and buy just the amount they want." She grins proudly as she watches us walk through the store.

On the counter is a box of small packages, each one with a picture of black squares. "Try some," she offers. "They're a breath candy called Sen-Sen." The lozenges are about half the size of my smallest fingernail. I pop one in my mouth. It has an intense licorice taste.

A white man comes in and uses a pay phone on the wall near the door. He puts coins in before he dials. Each clinks and falls into the phone's black catch box. "Most folks in this neighborhood don't have telephones," Aunt Myra explains.

Next to the cash register is a refrigerator loaded with popsicles and soft drinks. A handwritten sign taped to the front glass door reads: *Five cent return deposit on all soda bottles*. Coca-Cola is one of the soft drinks.

"Please, help yourself to a soda, honey child," Aunt Myra tells me.

"May I have one?" James asks.

"Sho'nuff. Y'all must be thirsty after your long trip."

I look at my choices. Michael picks one and shows Aunt Myra. She nods. "It's up to your mama."

"Boys, take just one," she says. Her "I mean business tone" and a raised eyebrow keep me from grabbing several.

Aunt Myra leads us out of the store to the back of her house. Phillip and Michael take off their shoes and socks and walk sideways on the grass, heel toe, heel toe.

Aunt Myra laughs. "*They* seems to know where they's goin'."

Around the corner, there's an old, sun-bleached rail fence running alongside the road as far as I can see. James points to a low, narrow, green building with three, screened openings. "A chicken coop," he says. "Let's look inside. I bet these chickens lay eggs, don't they, Aunt Myra?"

Different from our chicken coop back home, hers has rows of shelves with cubby holes side-by-side for the hens to lay their eggs. She reaches in under a hen and lifts out an egg. "See, boys? We got one."

Phillip, skipping ahead, turns around and runs back to us. "Look!" he shouts in surprise. "She has a vegetable garden back here!"

"Yeah, that's mah garden patch." Aunt Myra stops at the fence to survey what's growing. "Right there is the collards. Ain't them leaves big? And over there is the sweet potatoes."

Dad points to a tall, rectangular wooden building with two wide planks on the ground that lead to a door with a crescent-moon carving. "And that is an outhouse."

"Let's go in," James suggests.

"Not now, boys, unless you need to use it."

"What's it for?"

Dad laughs. "All right, go ahead and look inside."

"Can I go?" I ask.

"It might get crowded but…" He pauses and looks at me for a second. "Yeah, all of you, go with him." He motions the rest of my brothers to follow James and me. I detect a slight grin. "Be sure to take a deep breath."

Aunt Myra and Mom duck their heads, suppressing smiles.

I rush along the planks and pull the door open. My brothers and I crowd inside. It's small, dark, and stinky. I can make out a seat with two holes, kind of like a double toilet. I'm the first to back out. "*Phew!* The smell!"

"Just sit there and let it fall in," James says from inside.

"Let me out of here," Phillip says, pounding on the door.

Mom and Dad hold hands, laughing hard. Aunt Myra claps her hands over her mouth, snorts, and doubles over.

Charles asks, "Daddy, is that what we have to use to go potty?"

"I'd rather use the bathroom in your house," I say.

Aunt Myra looks at Dad.

"I'm afraid that's the only bathroom here," he tells us. "You'll have to wait a long time, if you want to use one in the house."

"Don't you have one inside?" Phillip asks Aunt Myra.

"No. A few folks in town do, but purtnear everybody has outhouses."

"I like your farm," I tell Aunt Myra.

She smiles. "Yeah, I love it here." She ruffles my hair.

We go to the front and enter her house. The living room inside is neat, clean, and comfortable, with a brown loveseat and matching sofa. White lace curtains dress the windows. On a stand near the window lies an open Bible with a black-leather cover, worn edges, and a long, red ribbon hanging down. A small free-standing bookcase has interesting-looking books. I scope out her high rocking chair to sit in and read when I have free time. "May I sit in your rocking chair?" I ask.

"Sho." Aunt Myra nods. "But first, I'll show y'all where to sleep, and you can put y'all's things away."

The bedroom has two windows. One looks out at the tree-lined road and the shaded houses farther down the way. The other opens onto the porch that stretches across the front of the house.

"Y'all boys will sleep here." She motions to a full-size bed.

"We're all sleeping in the same bed?" I ask. "All six of us?"

"Yassuh, that's where y'all going to sleep." She leaves me standing by the window, staring at the bed.

HARD WORK AND A MYSTERY

18.

Our second morning in Winona, like the first, begins with roosters calling to the hens. Already, the temperature promises to be warmer than yesterday. Aunt Myra's and Dad's voices carry throughout the house. I find them in the kitchen.

"Want me to get wood for the stove?" Dad offers.

"Nah, I got it last night," says Aunt Myra. "Got some fresh eggs, too. How does that sound, with country bacon?"

"*Mm-mm,* sounds good." The edges of Dad's eyes crinkle in that special way that tells me he's happy.

"Gaylloyd, hand me the iron poke on the hook above your head," she says. She inserts the tool in the plate on the stovetop, pours kerosene on the wood, and puts the plate back. She opens a rectangular side door then sticks in a lit wooden match. There's a big whoosh as the fuel lights. In no time, the room fills with smells of fried bacon, eggs, potatoes, and onions. The aromas lure Mom and my sleepy brothers into the kitchen.

After breakfast, I go outside to kick the can with a few neighborhood kids, who make fun of my clumsiness. Brown and speckled chickens roam everywhere throughout the green cornstalks. Barefoot children make a ruckus, playing another game in the cornfield with two of my brothers. Since we've been here, mostly negro folks come in and out of the store all day, to buy stuff. But this morning, two white women drive up with bundles of clothes. I leave the field and follow them into the store. Taped on the window is a hand-lettered sign: *Deliver dirty clothes by nine a.m.*

Inside, Dad takes the women's bundles. "Yes, ma'am, next week." They don't ask him for a receipt as they turn to leave. "Thank you," he says, but they don't reply.

"Hi, Dad." I greet him.

"I'm glad you came in. Mom and Aunt Myra are in the back, washing clothes. Aunt Myra works from sunup to sundown, and Mom's helping her. I want you to help."

"What can I do?"

"Ask Aunt Myra. I'm sure she'll appreciate your offer."

I didn't realize how much is involved in doing laundry by hand. Mom used to have a wringer washer. She washed our clothes in the machine and then ran each piece through its wringer, to squeeze soapy water out of the fabric. She refilled the washer with rinse water and repeated the wringing until the water ran clear. Now, though, she does all that work at home with a modern washer and dryer.

No such luck for Aunt Myra. Outside the back of the store is an open concrete pad. Over a fire pit hangs a giant, black cauldron. The heat from the huge chunks of glowing charcoal beneath makes it difficult to stand close.

I ask Myra, "Can I help?"

She stands in front of one of three huge washtubs on a wooden table, scrubbing a bed sheet on a washboard. Another aluminum tub of water and already washed clothes sits between her and Mom, who is at the third washtub, twisting other clothes to wring out the rinse water. A wicker basket on a smaller table near her is full of clothes ready to be hung on a line.

"Fill the water pail and dump it into the pot," Aunt Myra tells me. "I need more heated water."

I look for a faucet and garden hose near the store.

"You know where the well is?" Mom points near the fence to a four-foot-round brick well with an open wood roof covered with moss and weeds. It has a bucket hanging on a thick rope, ready to be lowered.

I bring the full bucket back to Aunt Myra. It's pretty heavy.

"One more is all I need. Get that, then hang the things your mama's done wrung out."

While I'm hanging up wet laundry, Dad wanders out back. "No one's in the store," he says.

Aunt Myra lets a shirt on the washboard slide back into the sudsy water. "George, ain't nobody but me to do the work around here, nowadays. Emma, before George left for the city, he and his sista ran this here place."

"Not quite, Auntie," Dad says. "What about that time you told Sissy and me to stay out of the way?" He laughs. "You must remember threatening to take a switch to us, if we bothered you and Miss Merriweather, when she came by to pick up her laundry."

Aunt Myra laughs at the mention of the woman's name.

"You told us not to make any noise."

She chuckles again.

"Aunt Myra taught us sign language," he says to me, "so we wouldn't be a bother. That time, Sissy signed a joke. I tried not to laugh but giggled anyway." To imitate Miss Merriweather, Dad raises his voice. "'Oh, Myra, which one is the dummy?' she asked."

"'Both of them,' Aunt Myra told her."

All of us burst out laughing, Dad the loudest.

The bell in the store rings.

"I'll get that," says Mom.

Aunt Myra strums the washboard with a white shirt. "Well, George, y'all was a big help. Always had a good head for numbers and a hard worker, you is. Now, they ain't nobody but me doin' the countin' and the record-keeping about what comes and what goes."

Mom comes back from the store. "Aunt Myra, Miss Billie Lou Noble says she has a gift for you and doesn't mind waiting on the porch at the house 'til you're ready."

"I haven't spoken to that woman since she put that spell on my cow, Geraldine. She been dry ever since. It'll be a long time before I'm finished here and ready to talk to that woman."

It is over two hours before we finish the wash and go back into the house through the kitchen. "I gonna see what Billie Lou wants with me," Aunt Myra says, and we follow her into the living room. She opens the front door and looks out through the screen.

Billie Lou, a pleasant-looking woman in a lavender-flowered cotton dress, sits on the porch swing, holding a pie in her lap.

"Hello, Billie Lou. How's y'all doin'?"

"Myra, dis here pie is 'specially for you," she says with a nod. "T'aint for nobody else, you hear?" She shakes her head. "Don't share dis pie with no one, not even your boy, George. I baked it only for y'all."

Aunt Myra opens the screen door and takes the pie.

"Now go ahead and have some," she adds.

"Oh, no, I ain't ate and don't want to spoil my supper. But don't worry. I'll have some later." Aunt Myra carries the pie into the house and places it on the dinner table. On her return to the porch, she whispers to Dad, "Dewberries. They hide poison." Back at the door, she says, "Billie Lou, thank you very much, but y'all just run along, hear me now?"

"But Myra, I been awaitin' all this time. I wants to see how much you like the taste and tell you how I done made it."

"Much obliged, Billie Lou, but my kin's here. You go on home now." Aunt Myra looks to the cloudless evening sky. "You know how it's gettin' dark and all."

"Yes, ma'am. And remember what I done told you. That pie is just for y'all." She sighs and looks inside over Aunt Myra's shoulders then turns to go. "You must be right about it gettin' dark. I may as well be goin' home."

Aunt Myra watches Billie Lou leave. When I go to the window after a while, Billie Lou is out of sight. Aunt Myra jumps as if startled, hurries to the table, and lifts the pie. "No tellin' what she done put in that there pie." She turns it in her hand, studying it. She looks at everyone in the room and says, as if we hadn't heard her the first time, "Specially made *just for me*!" Indeed. She done gone and put somethin' poison in it, I betcha."

The pie smells of fresh, sweetened dewberries. I try to imagine Billie Lou, so nicely dressed and appearing to be a kindhearted, sweet-talking country woman, poisoning a pie, and bringing it to Aunt Myra's house.

"Murder! That's murder. She'll go to jail." She turns it, slowly inspecting the crust's edges. "Gaylloyd, come here." She hands me the suspected pie. "I want you to take this to the outhouse and drop it in." She follows me to the kitchen door.

I go down the back stairs and across the planks, carrying it inside the outhouse. I hear the plate hit bottom. When I come out, Aunt Myra is at the back door, watching.

When I return, Dad looks up from a newspaper. "Auntie thinks the pie is poisoned," I tell him.

"Consider the evidence." He smiles and, folding the paper, says, "Don't believe everything you hear."

AN ATYPICAL DAY

19.

I swing open the kitchen door. Mom and Aunt Myra sit on tall stools in the corner, and Dad is standing by the stove with a cup of coffee.

"Dad, good morning."

He turns. "Good morning, son."

"Can I light the stove?"

"Do you know what to do?"

"Load the stove with wood, pour on kerosene, and light it," I say with an assured grin on my face.

"Go ahead."

"I'll wake the boys," Mom says.

I lift the iron plates to load the stove with wood, but before I'm finished, Dad and Aunt Myra leave the room, discussing something.

I pack in wood and pour kerosene on every piece until it puddles in the catch pan. With the cover plates secured, I pinch my nose and peek through the side door. The glistening wood boosts my confidence that a spectacular fire will soon heat the stove.

"Perfect. I'll watch the flames through the side door." I always feel important when I do things for Dad.

I study the matchstick's red-and-white tip and strike it on the side of the cast-iron stove, like Aunt Myra does. It flares with a dazzling flame and sizzling sound. With caution, I slowly insert the match into the opening, ready to behold the beauty of wood on fire.

Flames billow out through the opening faster than I can pull away. Intense heat strikes my face, and the odor of burnt hair fills my nostrils. I grab my scorched head and fall back. My shrieks bring Dad and Aunt Myra rushing back.

"Oh, mah word! Sit here." Aunt Myra helps me off the floor and onto the stool in the corner.

Mom hurries to my side.

"Why didn't you wait until we got back?" Dad bellows.

Aunt Myra reaches into a cupboard over the stove and hands Mom some cocoa butter. "I need a cool, damp cloth," Mom tells her. Aunt Myra grabs a terry cloth towel and dips it in a bucket near the sink. Mom dabs my face with the cloth and then smooths cocoa butter on my stinging burns. "I hope that'll help keep your skin from blistering."

Dad hovers over me, tipping my head back to get a good look at my face. "Emma, his eyelashes and eyebrows are singed off."

I cringe as Mom touches my forehead where my eyebrows are supposed to be and gasps.

"Honey, he'll be alright," Dad says.

Mom shifts to make room for him, so he can get a better look at my head and face.

"All your hair is gone," he tells me. I think I hear him laugh but I'm not sure. "And the color… Your skin is maroon. It'll peel, but you'll be fine."

I keep my eyes tight shut.

"Open your eyes," he says.

"Is there a doctor in this town?" Mom asks.

"He won't need one. Gaylloyd'll be alright," Dad says.

"There's soot in his eyes," she says. "I'll rinse them with water." She guides me to the sink.

James, who must have heard all the commotion, appears at the kitchen door, still in his pajamas. "What's wrong with Gaylloyd?" He sounds panicked. My other brothers show up.

After running water over my face, Mom walks me to the dining table, with my brothers close behind. One at a time, each one takes a look at me.

Phillip glances at his hand. There are splotches on it, with the color growing back. "You look like an ugly beet," he says.

Dad convinces me to stay on the porch because of the burns. Yesterday, I missed a whole day of play because of doing laundry, which wasn't exactly fun. Now, I can't go anywhere with the cocoa butter on my face and scalp. I get the Rudyard Kipling book Grandma gave me and sit on the swing suspended from the porch ceiling by a knotted rope. It creaks as I go back and forth, pushing my foot against the floor every once in a while, to maintain momentum. The salve soothes my skin, though it tingles.

The store's doorbell rings, and Aunt Myra comes out of the house.

"It's still morning and already hot today," I say.

"Hot? 'Taint hot, boy. After y'all been here in Winona a spell, you'll find out what a hot day is all about." She giggles to herself and hurries to the store.

The sway and crash of cornstalks and shouts of laughter pull my attention away from the book. My brothers are playing with other kids there. A slight young girl rushes up to the house, away from the ruckus. Although I watch her approach the porch, her yelling startles me.

"Tell y'all kin to *stop chunkin' dem der rocks!* Y'all hear me?"

I can't understand her thick drawl, so I stand up to hear better. "What?"

"Tell y'all brothers to stop chunkin' dem der rocks." Without waiting to see if I've figured out what she's saying, she hurries across the road, disappearing inside a green house. The moment she's out of sight, Michael and James charge out of the field, giggling and throwing chunks of sod at each other.

"Hey, you guys," I say. "Stop chunkin' dem der rocks, whatever that means."

They stand in the middle of the road and look at me for a moment then laugh at each other. Michael picks up a rock and throws it at James. James disappears back into the field with

Michael following.

I pick up my book again, but before I can start to read, a young man pulls up in front of the store in a horse-drawn cart and carries a tall, heavy, metal container inside. I follow him.

"Brought you some milk, fresh from Desi," he says to Aunt Myra. With a look of pride, he sets it in the refrigerator.

"Hi, Jacob. Y'all's just in time. I'm almost out of milk." Aunt Myra hands him an empty box. "When you finds what you need, put them in here."

He thanks her, heads to the shelves, and starts shopping. "Hear tell there's goin' to be some rain tomorrow," he says. "Today, it's supposed to get up to ninety-four, maybe more." I smile at the rhyme.

"I'll say," Aunt Myra says.

Jacob takes his receipt, thanks her, and leaves.

"He lives with his parents," she tells me. "They're a big family. I make arrangements with his folks. It's good business."

The screen door slams, and Dad rushes in. "Glad you're here," he says. He's out of breath and grinning about something. "We're making ice cream. Call your brothers and meet me out back."

We gather at the table where we washed clothes the day before.

"Boys, I want you to pay close attention." He sets an aluminum canister on the table and pulls up a bench. We sit and watch him ladle milk, eggs, and vanilla into the barrel. Then, he sets it inside a wooden ice cream maker, fills it with crushed ice and rock salt, and inserts a handle into a socket.

"Turn the crank counterclockwise ," he demonstrates. "And in a few minutes, we'll have ice cream. Who wants to be first?"

My brothers and I all shout, "I do!"

"Gaylloyd, turn it this way." Dad places his hand over mine. We crank it together for a few seconds, churning the mixture. After a while, I switch arms, then James takes over until Dad tells him to stop.

He looks inside.

"Is it ice cream yet?" Michael asks.

He closes the lid. "Not yet."

Michael takes the handle next, then Phillip, and then Charles. Even Mark wants a turn. It takes longer than a few minutes, but when Dad checks again, he announces, "It's ice cream!"

Everyone cheers.

"I'll let you taste it, but we'll have more after dinner, before tonight's talent show."

We sing in a chorus, "*Awww.*"

THE TALENT SHOW
20.

Dad invites everyone who lives around Aunt Myra's to the talent show. They're relatives, childhood friends, and neighbors; everyone who knew him since he was crawling in the dirt.

"Here's Danny Joe with someone I don't know," Dad says. Danny Joe is a stout man about Dad's age with wiry, salt-and-pepper hair that's parted in the middle. "He's one of the kids I grew up with."

"Hello, George. How y'all doin'? Ain't seen you in a coon's age. This is Shirley Anne, my wife." She nods, her arms wrapped around his biceps as though, if she let go, he would lift off the ground and float away. Her skin is smooth, and her sleek hair is wavy. She doesn't have much meat on her bones but stands just as tall as Danny Joe.

"What y'all been up to since you left Winona?"

"I'm doing just fine," Dad says. "I'm glad you came. Shirley Anne, would you and Danny Joe like to take a look at my Packard?"

"Oh, no," she says. "We walked from a long way out. I'm goin' inside and sit a spell with Myra. You two enjoy yourself." She lets go of Danny Joe's arm, passes me on the stairs, and goes into the house, calling, "Myra" without knocking at the door.

I tail Dad as he leads Danny Joe to the car.

"Most of the folks around these parts don't even have a car," Danny Joe says. "If'n they do, it's a beat-up ol' jalopy, and everybody and their cousins use it. Folks in this neighborhood mostly get around on foot. Some ride horses or mules they's boss done give 'em, much like befo' y'all left. Not much changes around here."

"That's exactly why I want you to see my new Packard." The windows are down. "Take a look at the radio. There're buttons for each station. Push one and you get the one you want." Dad opens the driver's door, turns the key one click, pushes a button, and stands behind Danny Joe. They both stare at the dashboard, listening to a station.

"George, we ain't got but one station here. It's gospel music and sure sounds good on your radio, like we's in chu'ch."

Dad pokes a few more buttons to change the channels but gets only static. He gets in, turns the radio off, starts the engine, and gets back out. He lifts the hood, and they watch the engine idle.

"Sho is good lookin', this here car."

"Don't need to shift gears, either. It's automatic. Get in. We'll go down the road a piece."

They pull away but are never out of my sight. Dad drives through the neighborhood until I almost can't see them then turns around, comes back, and stops near the front gate. Because other friends came earlier, this is his third roundtrip since this morning.

Afterward, as they walk around the car, Danny Joe kicks all four wheels. "George, I sure like it. Yessiree, I do. One of these days I's getting me a green one like y'all's. Sho'nuff, it must be a good thing where you live. Y'all gonna tell me about California, ain't you?"

"Why, of course. Come on inside. Let's see what our women folk are up to."

I follow them. Shirley Anne kisses Danny Joe when we enter. Aunt Myra says, "Danny Joe, it's near supper time. Your wife said y'all will eat with us."

Danny Joe chuckles then leans down and says to me, "Myra known me all my life."

Dad finds a place at the table for the three of us. They jaw jack about our drive here and the day's upcoming event. Mom, Aunt Myra, and Shirley Anne set two platters at opposite ends of the table, each brimming with roasted chickens carved as if they were turkeys. To make it easy to select a preference, the dark meat covers one end of the platters and white meat the other.

"Well, I guess we're ready. Chow's on," announces Aunt Myra, mopping her forehead with her apron.

Mom tells me, "Get your brothers to come in, wash up, and have a seat."

Once we are settled at the table, I pass the mashed potatoes to Dad, and he hands me a bowl of cream gravy. The mustard greens and turnips, cooked to death for hours, are fished out of the pot liquor, the water the vegetables cooked in.

"This meal reminds me of the day the preacher stopped by unannounced," Dad says, "just as we were ready to eat."

"Oh, no, George. Don't tell them that story," Aunt Myra chides.

Dad smiles at her. "Of course, he accepted our invitation to join us," he says, "and insisted on blessing the food." Mimicking the preacher, he clears his throat and, with one eye shut and the other open, looks at everyone at the table as if checking that no one had left. He folds his hands, bows his head, and continues. "'O Lord,' he prays, 'look down in tender mercy on such generous hearts as these. Make us truly thankful. Amen.' And he shouts, '*Pass the possum, please!*'"

I jump, and so does everyone else, except Aunt Myra, who applauds. The rest of us laugh.

After the meal, Danny Joe stands. "Scrumptious," he says, rubbing his bulging stomach. "If I had room, I'd have a third helpin' of them greens with more of that pot liquor."

My brothers, Danny Joe, and Dad go outside, dragging their feet across the wood floor as if shouldering a heavy load from eating too much. I leave the table carrying half the dirty dishes to the kitchen.

"Y'all sure burnt your face bad," Shirley Anne says. I hand her the dishes and return to the table for the rest. "Oh, go on outside with y'all's daddy. He needs your help more than I do."

From the porch, which will be the talent show stage, I see neighbors already waiting on the lawn, laughing, and milling around. The families who arrived while we were eating have found places on the grass or settled under the catalpa tree. The big, green, heart-shaped leaves are scattered around. Fragrant white flowers cover the ground like cotton. A few kids swing as high as they dare on the tire swing. Others jump off a huge bouncy limb that hangs close to the ground. More amble toward the house with smaller children in hand or walk around, visiting friends with their parents. Everyone is nicely dressed for the occasion in their Sunday-go-to-meetin' clothes. Men and boys wear slacks and button-down shirts. At least half wear hats. Women and girls are in colorful summer dresses or blouses with skirts. Nearly everyone fans themselves. I'm glad Mom told us to dress up; otherwise, we'd still be in our play clothes.

Mom and Aunt Myra come out of the house and sit in the swing with Mark and Charles on their laps. Two gray-haired ladies settle on chairs nearby and sip lemonade.

"I knowed y'all's daddy when he didn't know if he's a comin' or a goin'," one says to me, "And just look at him now."

"Praise the Lord," says the other.

"And I 'member the day he done left here to join the Navy, and later he comes back all married up with y'all, just to visit," the other tells Mom.

Mom and I smile and nod our heads.

Dad hustles about on the porch, setting up his new toy: a reel-to-reel tape recorder the size of a suitcase and so heavy, he leans backward to carry it. He places it on a table outside the door and connects it to an outlet in the house using an extension cord he packed with our luggage. "This very well may be the first time any of my friends here have seen one of these contraptions," he tells me.

He picks up the microphone and strides back and forth, dragging its long black cord across the floor. "Testing one, two, three," he says.

He admits he likes getting attention—a ham, he says. When his ship is at sea, he entertains officers and sailors alike. When he's in San Diego, he performs at the Old Globe Theater. Today, as the Master of Ceremonies for our show, he asks all the participants to use the mic.

He introduces James first. "James, will you come to the porch?" A girl laughs as he passes her... "Tell everybody something about yourself."

James takes the mic. "Well, I'm in the Boy Scouts. Our school had a dance this spring. I helped catch the chickens that Dad and Mom cooked for our meals before we drove all the way across the United States." My brother isn't shy, so Dad cuts him off with a gesture. "Just one more thing, Dad. I saw a snake at the picnic grounds in Arizona." He hands the mic back.

"James, thank you." The crowd claps, and he dips his head toward them. "Son, what are you going to sing for us today?"

"'Ave Maria.'" Dad hands him the mic. James positions himself on the top step and begins singing a cappella. His clear boy-soprano voice holds the high notes beautifully and so clear, it makes me tear up.

A man standing near me whispers, "He sings like an angel. Even the babies listen."

When James finishes, many in the crowd jump to their feet, clapping and shouting, "Hallelujah" and "Praise the Lord." He smiles broadly and bows over and over. He never gets that kind of response back home, so I'm pleased to see him receive accolades for something he's done well.

Dad beams. "Well done, James. It's not easy to follow an opening act like that," he says to everyone else. "But I have a Paul Laurence Dunbar poem for you today. I'm sure you've heard of 'When Malindy Sings.' It's my favorite. It goes like this..."

> "G'way an' quit that noise, Miss Lucy–
> Put that music book away;
> What's the use to keep on tryin'?
> If you practice until you're gray,
> You cain't start no notes a-flyin'

Like the ones that rants and rings
From the kitchen to the big woods
When Malindy sings."

The poem's narrator is shocked that Miss Lucy has never heard Malindy sing. He tells her, "The fiddler forgets to fiddle, and the mockingbird stops trying to whistle."

Dad also gets huge applause and takes several swooping bows like a musketeer. Next, he introduces Carolina, a cousin of ours. She's short, dark, and plump with chin-length hair pressed straight and neat bangs cut an inch above her eyebrows.

"Have you lived here all your life?" Dad asks.

"Nassuh, not yet," she jokes, getting chuckles from the audience.

"That's a good one, Carolina." He winks at Mom. "What are you going to do for us today?"

"A *pahm*," she says, in the southern-Mississippi vernacular I still don't understand.

"Carolina is going to recite a poem for us," Dad announces as he hands her the mic. I'm grateful for his clarification.

She positions herself in the center of the porch, faces the audience, and, with a lilting voice, begins. "Fo Gotsa lub da wod, Hep gape ed hiz oinly sa-un, fo Hep wa da oinly wo-un."

I don't understand a word of her poem. She curtsies to hearty applause and praise, hands the microphone to Dad, and bounces down the steps to rejoin her family on the lawn.

After her, everyone who wants to dance, sing, quote scripture, or otherwise perform takes their turn. The sky is almost dark when the last of the guests say their final goodnights, and fireflies light their way back home.

None of us are able to sleep that night. My brothers and I lie in bed, listening to the recording of Carolina's poem. Finally, when we hear it for the sixth time, I figure it out. It's from the Bible. "For God so loves the world, He gave us His only son, for He's the only one." I get it! This has been one of the best days of our trip.

THE MOVIE

21.

Moseying out of the hot morning sun into the house, I greet a girl rocking in Aunt Myra's chair. A smile lifts her cheeks.

"Good morning." She turns slightly to better see me, her straightened hair shifting on her shoulders. "Myra asked me to wait here for y'all. How y'all doin' today?"

Though she's wearing a green gingham pinafore today, I recognize her as the girl who wanted my brothers to stop chunkin' rocks. I'm at a loss for a reply, other than, "Fine."

I watch her rock back and forth, hands on the handles and feet on the rockers. Her erect posture makes her look as if she's struggling to appear grown up. "My name's Hattie. I live in the house over yonder. I saw you yesterday. Your brother sure has a good singin' voice."

"I'm Gaylloyd. You should hear him sing in church. ."

"Sho, I know your name. I come by to ask if you and your brothers want to go to the picture show."

"I'm sure they will. I'll ask my parents. Who else is going?"

"My brother, Wally."

"Are we going to sit in the balcony?" I've always wanted to sit up there. In San Diego, Mom always goes to the theater with us. She likes the seats downstairs, but my friends say the balcony has the best ones.

"In the balcony?" Hattie looks at me as if I've asked something she's never considered. "Sho'nuff. I'll be back in about an hour."

I hold the door open for her to step out onto the porch. "Good. We'll be ready."

After getting permission, I call my brothers. Only the four oldest can go. We wait on the porch for Hattie.

When she arrives, she's with her brother, Wally. "What happened to your eyebrows?" she asks. "You born that way?"

"No." I describe the accident.

Hattie laughs. "Sure looks funny."

I don't like being told I look funny, so I change the subject, and we all start walking toward town. "My mom and dad talked a lot about the presidential race before the elections. Did you want Eisenhower or Stevenson to win?"

"What elections?"

"You know—the presidential elections! My folks voted for Eisenhower. He won."

"You're funnin' me, ain't you? You say funny things."

I can't figure out why she doesn't know about Eisenhower. "He was a general in the war. My dad said he served with him. Who did your parents vote for?"

"I don't think they's ever voted. No one I knows has ever heard about votin'. I never heard nothin' about no votin'."

I'm amazed she knows nothing about voting or the last presidential election. I was seven at the time of the elections and followed the whole thing on the radio. I listened to the discussions between Mom and Dad and my aunt and uncle. In school, even our teachers, the nuns, talked about it. "Don't you learn about these things in school?"

"We has our readin', writin', and 'rithmetic. Ain't that what you learn?"

"Yeah, we study those things, but this year, we also had civics, where we learned about our country."

"You sure comes up with lots of newfangled words and things I never heard about. Y'all must have those things out there in California, don't you?" She looks away then walks faster, kicking the dirt with her toes.

Doing my best to keep up with her and be considerate of her feelings, I change the subject again. I tell her about my friends, Uncle Arthur's family, and the long drive through different states to get here. She doesn't slow down but focuses all her attention on the direction we're heading. I try to think of something she might be interested in, so I point out the golden pears on the tree in the front yard of the house we're passing.

Aunt Myra's fence keeps chickens in the coop and pests out of her garden. But near as I can tell, this home's fresh-painted white picket fence, manicured lawn, and bright flowers along the walkway are just for looks. I stop at the fence's gate, in front of the pear tree. Its branches touch the ground under the weight of the fruit.

Everyone except Hattie huddles around me. "*Mmmm*, those pears sure smell sweet," I say. "They look ripe enough to eat."

"Our neighbors at home share the figs on their trees," James tells Wally. "There are more than enough pears here. I'm picking one." He goes into the yard.

The tree's fullness beckons me to follow. "Take only one."

"Get one for me!" Wally shouts.

While we're in the yard, Hattie stands with her brother, biting her lips. She shakes her head as I pick a second one for Wally and bite into mine. "This neighborhood seems really different from where you and Aunt Myra live. Are the people around here rich?"

"Did y'all see that old white woman lookin' out the window?" Hattie asks.

"No."

Hattie doesn't say any more, but I can tell she's upset. She walks away. I hurry to catch up. She looks hard at me as I take another bite.

"Y'all shouldn'a done that without asking." Her pace quickens, so we have to run to keep up with her.

On the main street in town, we can easily see all the stores from one end to the other. We casually follow Hattie off the sidewalk onto the road. All the people going in and out of the barber shop, a clothing store, and a lawyer's office ignore us. The Upton Theater, a beige, stucco building, is on a corner in the center of Winona. In the slow line to the ticket window, families and couples talk and laugh with one another.

I think we will join the line, but Hattie leads us around to the back of the building. We stop at the bottom of a rusted metal staircase that looks like a fire escape.

"Y'all just wait here while I get tickets," she says to us. "I won't be long."

"I'll go with you," I say.

"No, you needn't." She leaves us there and returns to the front.

A family glances at us and climbs the stairs. The father smiles, says howdy to Wally, then directs his children up to the top. Hattie's gone for a long time. James tags Phillip then falls on the ground to avoid a return tag, but Phillip tags Michael. More people climb the stairs. "I think I should check why she's not back," I tell James.

"No, she's coming."

Phillip runs up to me. "I'm thirsty."

"You'll have to wait until we get inside." I don't know how long we wait. I finally see Hattie coming around the corner from the front. She hands ticket stubs to each of us. "These'll prove that y'all's ticket is paid for."

Fidgeting, squeezing his legs together, and holding his groin, Michael says, "Hattie, I have to go to the bathroom."

"Y'all has to wait 'til we git inside. The movie starts in a minute. There is nowhere down here where y'all can go. Come on. Follow me." She climbs the stairs then waits at the weathered gray door on the landing. It's cracked and peeling, with the words *Fire Escape* barely visible above.

As Hattie opens it, its hinges creak. "Y'all have to lift the door to keep it from coming off," she explains.

"It's been a long time since it was painted," James says.

Hattie holds the door open.

I hurry to get out of the sun. "I've always wanted to sit in the balcony," I tell her.

"I sho don't know why," she answers, then shows Michael a room just off the fire escape. "Here's the bathroom."

He tries the door. It's open.

"I'll be finished in a minute," says a lady from inside.

He pushes it shut. "Is there another one?"

"No."

The woman comes out, leaving the door ajar.

"This is for girls," he complains.

"There ain't no boy one," Hattie says with a laugh. "Y'all best hurry before a girl comes."

When my eyes finally adjust to the dark, I see metal folding chairs propped against the walls. Others are lying on the dusty floor, with a few arranged haphazardly near the railing. The hot room smells musty. The floor angles sharply down to a banister. I balance myself, make it to the railing, and look over. The seats below are plush, and many are empty. The carpets, like the cushioned chairs, are red velvet. Only white people are down there.

"I want to go downstairs," Phillip tells Hattie. "It looks much better than up here."

Me, too, I want to say. And there's plenty of room for us downstairs. I think of Memphis and of my Cousin Lee explaining why those kids chased us. He said that white and colored folks don't like one another. Maybe it's also true here.

"Y'all can't sit down there." Hattie's tone makes it final.

I grab a chair and sit as close to the railing as possible. James finds a place on one side of me, and Michael and Phillip sit on the other. The slope of the floor makes sitting uncomfortable.

The movie is *The Girl Can't Help It*, with Hollywood actress Jayne Mansfield. I'm soon laughing until my sides ache. Whenever her curvy figure and long legs catch the attention of any male, an accident occurs. Half-blind men's eyeglasses crack, shatter, or fall off their faces. Small boys playing marbles gawk at her and allow their marbles to spill out of the bag. Male drivers crash into trees and light poles. Older boys fall off their bicycles or plow into pedestrians.

For a while, the movie makes me forget about the balcony's

condition. Back home, the guys brag about the balcony and always take their girlfriends up there. I'm sure none of the movie theaters at home are like this one.

As we leave after the movie, I wonder why negroes are upstairs and white folks sit downstairs, but I don't mention it.

We're still laughing at funny parts of the show when we near the house with the pear tree. Hattie looks around carefully. She grabs Wally's and Phillip's hands and hurries away from the house on a different route.

"What's the matter?" I ask her.

"Those people standin' in that there yard where y'all got the pears, well, white folks live there."

"*Uh-huh*," I say.

"Well, I think we better go home another way."

"My cousin in Memphis says it's different there than where I live. I'm beginning to think Winona might be like where he lives."

"I don't know about Memphis. Never been there. Isn't where y'all lives like here?"

"No." I try to describe my home to her.

"Well, this ain't California," she says.

The differences between San Diego and Winona make me yearn to be back home. I'm even more confused here than I was in St. Louis. Because Dad grew up here, he says he's home now. "I'm only a visitor in your town," I tell Hattie.

She stops walking and looks at me for a long moment. "In Mississippi, y'all has to stay in your place. Y'all don't belong here." She turns and leaves me.

She's right. I don't belong here. This place makes me feel like a misfit.

BELIEFS

22.

The next morning, I'm coming out of my room when Aunt Myra, still in her nightgown, shoves me out of her way and scurries past me onto the porch.

"What's the matter?" I call to Aunt Myra and join Mom, following her outside.

"I don't know what she's upset about. I was fixing breakfast when she rushed in, grabbed a jar of bay leaves, and rushed out in a tizzy," Mom tells me.

Someone has left nine dolls made of cloth and stuffed with hay on the front steps. One doll reclines against each step's rise, facing away from the house. Six are small, three are large. Their heads are pale, with green dots for eyes and noses, but they have no mouth or arms. Two large ones are in blue dresses, one on the bottom step and the other in the middle. The third large doll sits on the floor against the railing at the top of the porch, facing the front door. Like the six smaller dolls, it wears coarse beige pants.

Aunt Myra sings long and harsh to the three large dolls and tosses handfuls of bay leaves on the stairs. "I knows who done this!" she mutters, as she lets more bay leaves fall from her fingers around each of the smaller figures. After looking down the road and shouting, "*Billie Lou*," she throws the rest of the leaves over her head into the air. Whatever she's doing, the ritual has a powerful meaning to her.

She leaves the yard and hurries toward the barn. I lean on the rail to watch her. Chickens in her path squawk and scatter. One red hen flies over the gate just as she opens it.

Mom and I step down into the yard to get a better look at each cross-legged burlap figure. Their eyes seem to focus on us. "What's she doing?" I ask.

"I don't know. I wish your dad were here. Where is he?"

Before long, Aunt Myra comes back, still chanting. Phillip and Charles are right behind her and she carries a bunch of flowers in her hand, each flower wrapped with a white ribbon. Me, Mom, and my brothers follow her up the steps.

I put my finger to my lips. "Don't say anything."

We all watch as Aunt Myra lays the flowers around the big doll at the top. When she's finished, she goes back down to the bottom step, looking wild-eyed. She stares at the doll sitting there, screams at it, stomps once in front of it, then sings, "*Lukumi Yemaya*," twirls, rushes at it, and then backs away.

We're joined by James and Dad, who's carrying Mark. Dad leans toward Mom and whispers, "Voodoo."

She nods and pulls me closer. I'm mortified. The nuns say pagans believe in voodoo. In catechism class, they collect five dollars to help missionaries save them. I can't believe my Aunt Myra is a pagan.

Aunt Myra pauses for a moment, inhales deeply, and then swaggers to the smaller doll on the next step and begins again. Her dance is smooth. Her song is soft and comforting, like a lullaby. I don't recognize the words. The language could be either her father's Choctaw or her mother's Hadzabe. I figure, because their size and clothes are different, the six smaller dolls represent my brothers and me, while the larger dolls signify Aunt Myra, Mom, and Dad. She never glances at us during this time.

She gathers flowers around the doll at the top of the stairs and pulls their petals off. With tears in her eyes, she lays the stems down. When she completes her pagan antics, Aunt Myra tiptoes down to the first step, strikes a match, and chants, "*Lukumi Yemaya*" again, and lights the straw stuffing of each doll, one by one. As they burst into flame, she sings raucous tunes. She ascends one side of the stairs, twirling in a new dance, and descends on the other side. We watch in silence until nothing remains but ashes and charred spots on the staircase.

Aunt Myra looks less dazed. She brushes soot from her nightgown, walks up to Dad, smiling, and says, "Well, that should handle it. Y'all hungry?"

* * *

Late that evening, I'm settled in the rocking chair, my favorite place in the front room, enjoying its back-and-forth motion while I read. I have three books in my lap: two that I brought with me plus the one Grandma gave me.

My brothers lie on their stomachs on the rug, reading their own books, their feet dancing in the air. The lighting over their shoulders comes from two kerosene lamps on the table.

Aunt Myra leans over the Bible, studying a verse. Every once in a while, she reads something aloud, trying to memorize it.

She has the nicest house in her neighborhood, but her furniture is old and worn. Electrical wiring runs between exposed roof rafters. Five bare lightbulbs dangle from the ceiling joists. One is centered in the front room, while two more hang in the kitchen and dining room. Another is nailed over the front door on the porch, and a fifth shines from the back stairs onto the wooden planks leading to the outhouse. Tonight, all the bulbs are off, so only the waning half-moon lights the way to the outdoor toilet. Paying attention to my book while eavesdropping on my parents' discussion at the same time is hard. I read the same paragraph more than once.

"I knew nothing about Catholics when I was growing up," Dad says.

"Yes, George," Mom replies. "And you know what people say around here isn't true."

"That's for sure. I heard when a nun smiles at you, your teeth will fall out of your mouth." He laughs. "Once, I went to the store downtown, and as I walked in, a nun turned and smiled at me. I covered my mouth, bowed my head, and left. I still had my teeth the next week, so I felt like I'd made it out of there in the nick of time."

I laugh and lay my book on my lap. "Oh, Dad."

"That's what they say about nuns around here. The first time I ever set foot in a Catholic Church was on a date with your mother. I couldn't get over how everyone stood, sat, and kneeled, over and over, during the whole Mass. The priest turned, spread his arms, and spoke in a strange language. I had no idea what he was saying, but suddenly the people stood. Then he'd say something else, and they'd kneel."

"I hadn't thought about how you'd never been to a Mass. I should have told you they're always in Latin." Mom sits on the couch.

"Remember, Emma? I was dressed in my best suit, fresh from being professionally pressed at the cleaners. All through the Mass, I worried about how the kneeling would wrinkle my slacks and take out those expensive creases."

Mom chuckles, and Dad says to me, "Your mom took a train to Seattle, where we were married. I was sure I'd have to fight the priest after our wedding."

"Why is that?" Mom scoots over to let me sit next to her.

"People here in Winona claim Catholic priests have first rights to the wedding bed. There is no way I would stand for that."

"Dad, what does that mean?" I ask.

"I didn't think you really believed that," Mom says, looking alarmed. She pats my knee. I sense it's not a good time for me to ask what he's talking about.

"I knew nothing about Catholicism until I took catechism classes. That was after James was born."

Aunt Myra snorts and rolls her eyes at him.

Headlights flash in the window, and a car pulls up next to ours. Dad walks to the door with Aunt Myra and me on his heels.

Moonlight filtering through the catalpa tree lights the way for a man in a dark suit, with a reverse collar, and a black Stetson. He walks to the porch with some kind of a satchel in his hands.

Aunt Myra turns on the light and opens the door before he knocks. "May I help y'all?"

"Good evening. I'm Father Monahan. Just stopping by to say hello and welcome George and his family to our humble town."

Aunt Myra storms off into the kitchen as Dad invites the visitor in. Seconds later, I hear the back door close with a loud bang. Dad ignores it, makes introductions and offers him a chair.

"A parishioner told me you were in town," Father Monahan says. "I'd like to talk about Sunday Mass. Did you receive my letter?"

"Yeah, the day before we left. Just a minute." Dad goes to the back and returns, reading the letter to himself.

"Is Sacred Heart church far from here?" Mom asks.

"The drive is about ten minutes from here, ma'am. It's just a bit on the other side of town."

The priest opens his satchel. "This is the letter you sent to the church."

Dad lays both letters on the Bible stand. Before leaving San Diego, Dad wrote, asking permission to attend church:

> Dear Father Monahan,
>
> We are a Catholic family of eight visiting my aunt, Myra Moore. I have never known a negro family to attend service in the church in Winona, and I'm concerned about our spiritual needs and obligations. If Catholic negroes are not allowed to attend your church, where may we go to Mass?
> With great respect, I implore you to quickly advise.
> Sincerely,
> George Upton Sissón

The priest wrote back:

Dear Mr. Sissón,

Thank you for your letter. Everyone knows Myra Moore. I announced to the congregation that your family will visit, and they insist that you attend Mass at our church in Winona. I personally wish to welcome you and your family. Please let me know when you arrive.

Sincerely,

Father Monahan

"Our Masses are at nine and ten in the mornin'," says Father Monahan, "and we'd be honored to have y'all attend."

"We usually attend the nine o'clock," Mom says.

"I'm happy to hear that." He stands and heads for the door. "I'll be expecting your family Sunday at 9. Sorry I can't stay longer. It's late, and I still have several things to do tonight."

Mom and Dad walk him to the door. "Father Monahan, thank you for stopping by," says Mom.

"My pleasure, ma'am."

Aunt Myra comes into the room as soon as his car pulls away. "I'm sorry, but I gots things to do in the store. What did that man want?"

"He came by to tell us that we're welcome to come to church this Sunday," Mom says.

"Well, if y'all listen to me, honey, I wouldn't go there. No good comin' out of those Catholic chu'ches." She looks at Mom.

"Aunt Myra," she says, dismay on her face. She sits on the couch, puts her head down, and places her hands on the sides of her temples. Then she looks up at Dad and me.

"It's a good thing the priest visited us," Dad says to his aunt. "We're a Roman Catholic family. Mass is the holiest event for us. It's the apex of our understanding of Christ's purpose for coming to Earth to save mankind."

Aunt Myra walks to the middle of the room with her hand on her hip and looks at him.

"The church is important to us. In San Diego, we even send our children to a Catholic school," Mom adds.

Aunt Myra shakes her head. "I don't know. I just don't know. Ol' Miss Wilkinson is a white lady who comes to the store every mornin'. The day before y'all got here, she tole me all the letters from y'all are read at the post office before they delivers them. She says every white person in Winona knows y'all be a-comin'."

Mom puts an arm around Aunt Myra's shoulder.

"What she done tole me makes me wonder," Aunt Myra continues. "I 'spect somethin', 'cause the envelope is always open when I gets the checks from George. He's done sent me money every month since he joined the Navy."

I touch Mom's arm. "Mom, she can't believe that. People don't read other people's mail, do they? What kind of place is this?" Mom pulls me close to her, hugs me, and puts her index finger to her lips. I say nothing more.

"I keep my business to myself," Aunt Myra says, putting her hand on my shoulder. "No one would know y'all is a comin' until after y'all got here. The only way these white folks found out is by readin' my mail."

SATURDAY BATH AND SUNDAY MASS

23.

On Saturday night, everyone takes a bath whether they need one or not, another Dad joke. Aunt Myra uses the same aluminum wash tub for bathing as she does for clothes washing. I bring the tub in from outside and put it on the kitchen floor next to the stove. Myra and Mom heat kettles of water on the wood stove and pour them into the basin.

Because the youngest bathe first, followed on up in age to the adults, Mark and Charles get in the tub first. When the water gets dirty, James and I empty it out the back door and refill it with more warm water. James finishes his bath while I help Mom and Dad get my younger brothers ready for bed. Taking a bath in the warm, steamy kitchen, using homemade soap, is fun.

"Tomorrow's a big day," Dad tells us. "And I want you boys to be ready early."

Sternly, Mom adds, "After Gaylloyd is finished bathing, I want all of you in bed, and don't anyone get up 'til morning."

Stressing his name, Dad says, "Michael, stay in bed with your brothers, even if you wake up before they do."

Michael often gets up in the middle of the night and climbs in with Mom and Dad. He falls asleep before they realize he's there.

Dad has to carry him back and lie down with him until he goes to sleep again. Many times, Dad is too drowsy to make it back to his own bed.

The bay window in our bedroom looks out onto the front porch. We say our prayers and climb in bed. Like every other night since we got here, we chat about the relatives and neighbors we've met, the places we've discovered, and the things we've done.

Dad comes into the room to check on us. "Is everyone ready to go to sleep?"

"I have to go to the bathroom," Charles says.

"Who else needs to go?"

We all chime in. "I do."

"Okay, boys," Dad says in mock exasperation. "I want all of you to go, and when you get back, go to sleep. If I hear any more chatter after that, I'm going to wear out your behinds."

We go out the kitchen door, down the stairs, and along the planks to the outhouse. They're still wet from the bath water emptied earlier and glisten in the moonlight. Fireflies flit around, blinking on and off, and bullfrogs harrumph in the distance.

I'm still not used to the outhouse. The smell discourages any unnecessary visits, especially as a reading hideaway. It is built over a deep hole with double toilet seats that are so high, it's an effort to climb up.

James and I help our younger brothers to use the outhouse before we do. I have no fear or concerns about peeing into the opening, but when I have to sit, I worry about falling in. As I sit there, my legs dangling, I imagine snakes nipping my rump. The toilet paper is hooked on a spindle, almost out of reach. I've always taken flush toilets for granted and can't wait to use one again.

I rush back to the house behind my brothers, and we all climb into bed. Sleep is immediate. My dreams are a jumble of everything I did today.

* * *

Because this is the day we're attending Mass, I wake early. Mom finds James and me already dressed, our shoes polished, and helping our brothers. The shirts and ties Mom pressed for my siblings lie on the made-up bed.

"Eatin' breakfast before y'all goes to chu'ch?" Aunt Myra asks Mom.

"No, ma'am. We'll eat when we get back. We go to early Mass, so the kids don't need to fast too long. Catholics don't eat before taking Communion."

"Is that so? When do y'all expect to get back?"

"After ten o'clock," Mom says. "Mass is only an hour."

"Then I'll have some fixins for y'all."

Mom pins on the feathered hat with the blue-silk bow that she made especially for this occasion. She turns her head in the mirror to look at it from different angles. "How do you like it?"

"Right pretty," answers Aunt Myra, as she kisses her on the cheek and sends us out the door.

We arrive five minutes before Mass begins. The church is in town, on the other end of the street near the theater. As we drive through town, I see a few people walking to church but no dark-skinned people.

Dad parks, and we jump out at once. As we enter, four parishioners stand at the door. "Welcome to Sacred Heart Church," says a pleasant, gray-haired man. The woman next to him hands Mom a program. Dad leads us down the center aisle to near the front, and we sit in pews where the parishioners are seated, like at home, and wait for services to begin.

"There aren't many people here," James whispers to me.

I turn and look behind us. There are no more than twenty. "You're right, but this isn't a big church."

When we entered, I noticed we're the only children, but I quickly forget about that as soon as Mass begins. Everything is familiar to me, other than the fact that no other negroes or Mexicans are here.

The honey-colored pews gleam. Bright stained glass adorns the arched windows. The walls and ceiling are white. Father Monahan introduces us as special guests from California. During Communion, we stand up with the rest of the congregation and take the Sacramental Host, a small white disc of unleavened bread.

Mass ends after the priest says a few more prayers in Latin, blesses those attending, and sings a closing hymn. We sing along. Then the priest leaves the altar. We file out with the rest. Like at home, the priest stands at the door, visiting with people as they leave.

"Thanks for coming," he says to Dad and Mom, grasping their hands with both of his. "Please come back any time."

"Father, thank you so much for your hospitality," says Dad. "You certainly make us feel right at home."

"James, look at all the people waiting for the next Mass," I say. "Where are they all going to sit? There must be a hundred people there."

Our church in San Diego has five Sunday-morning Masses and one in the evening, each less than an hour. While I'm not surprised that people are already waiting to attend the next Mass, I am puzzled that there are way more than a hundred, especially since the church is so small.

"I don't think all those people will find a place to sit," I say.

"These people don't look like they're dressed for Mass. Maybe they're poor," James says, then skips away from me in a high-hop, jack-rabbit fashion, slipping between a tall, blonde girl holding hands with two very young boys and some of the other people standing on the sidewalk. "Let's go!" he shouts to us. "I'm hungry."

The teenage girl pulls her charges to the side. Mom and Dad nod and smile as they pass. My other brothers and I follow, jabbering about church.

Aunt Myra stands on the front porch to greet us when we return. Delicious aromas fill the air, and my tastebuds water even before I enter the house.

"How do bacon, eggs, and flapjacks sound to y'all?" she asks me, smiling at Dad. In the center of the dining table is a platter with dozens of golden disks and a plate piled high with bacon.

"Pancakes!" Michael cries.

"Oh, no, honey. These are flapjacks," she says. "I done made them with sweet potatoes and clabber milk. There's coffee for y'all," she says to Mom, "and milk for the boys."

"Can we eat now?" Michael asks.

"Of course, honey. Of course."

Our mouths are too busy to talk about church.

ARISE FROM THE DEAD
24.

After breakfast, I usually take a nap on the porch or enjoy an uninterrupted read as I ease the swing back and forth. This morning, Aunt Myra's newly arrived visitor enlivens the living room. She, Dad, and Mom crack up at everything he says.

I slip inside with a soda from the store to find out if what they're laughing about is something I want to hear.

"Come on in," Dad says when he sees me. "This is an old family friend, Jove. We are catching up on the town news."

Jove is lanky and about the same height as Dad, with a light complexion and brown freckles sprinkled across his cheeks and forehead. He looks like Abraham Lincoln with tight, curly hair and no beard. He wears a dark, too-small fedora and a nice striped shirt. A few of his upper teeth are missing, and his tongue keeps trying to position a set of partial dentures into place while he talks. He and Dad sit on the couch, with Mom and Aunt Myra in chairs across from them. Between them is a small table with cups of coffee, a milk pitcher, a sugar bowl, and toast on a saucer.

"Oh, yeah, Dad. I bet it's old-folks' talk." I help myself to a piece of toast and stand next to Mom.

"How is William doing?" Dad asks Jove.

"Lordy have mercy, mercy, mercy," Jove answers. He leans forward, chuckling, bobbing his head, and wringing his weathered hands. Everyone shakes their heads as if they know what he's going to say.

"Is it all right with y'all, Emma, if the boy sits right here next to me?" Jove pats the cushion between Dad and himself.

She nods.

He looks me in the eye before he begins his narrative. "What happened to We'yum is somethin' else. Y'all gots to hear every word I say, down to the end.

"We'yum been married to Tammie Mae for comin' on twenty-eight years. She was way older than him and meaner than a tied-up cat. She was right purty when We'yum met her, and he loved her more than anythin'. One thing about her that everybody agreed to is that she was a lazy woman. Some mornings, We'yum would go off to work almost without breakfast, because she told him she needed her beauty rest. If We'yum wanted breakfast, she wasn't gettin' up to fix it, she said, so he could fix it himself. And they lived this way for twenty-eight years, hear me?" He nods.

"After a long day pickin' cotton, he'd hurry home every day to help around the house. If she had gots out of bed, she would more than likely have not gotten out of her night clothes. The house was always dirty. If he asked her about housework, she'd pipe up, 'Y'all want it done, then do it yourself.' Which he do.

"All around her chair was cracker crumbs, chicken bones, and candy wrappers. She dropped them all day long while he'd be out there pickin' cotton. 'Clean up this mess,' she'd tell him, 'if y'all don't like it.' And when he done did that, he'd fix supper for their three children and then straighten up the toys they left layin' round the house. Lordy, I seen the place myself. Pigs wouldn't live there.

"All the time he be cleanin' up her mess, she be gossipin' about the other folks, like Ella Mae, Jessie, Sally Ann, or the preacher. Sho'nuff, there would be lots to say about them folks, and she be sayin' it."

Jove stops, takes a deep breath, and looks around at everyone. All of us are listening.

"One day, purt near three months ago, after all those years of marriage and when they children were all grown and gone,

Tammie Mae done up and died. We'yum felt he needed to do the right thing as he always done. He hired the best criers in town, everybody knows them."

Dad interrupts to explain how professional funeral criers are women who make sure everyone is cared for at a funeral. "They cater to the needs of grieving families and make sure food is brought to their homes. Dressed head to toe in black, they also lead the crying during wakes, which helps mourners express their emotions."

"Y'all right about that, George," Jove says. "The mortician did an excellent job of dressin' Tammie Mae's big old body. She had on a beautiful, brand-new, blue-and-pink lace dress with the fanciest hat I ever done seen." He looks at me and giggles. "Her lips were crimson red, and her cheeks were rouged. He almost made her look alive." Jove taps his feet on the wooden floorboards to the rhythm of his speech and gestures in the air with his skinny hands and arms.

"The mortician didn't have none of that embalmin' stuff, so it was necessary to have a quick funeral service and burial. He said he was afraid rigor mortis might set in.

"The funeral was that evening, the same day she done died. Everybody was der, sittin' in their pews at chu'ch. The preacher came out and stood in the pulpit above the coffin. While the criers were crying, he talked his head off about how everybody was gonna miss her so much. When he'd finished, different other folks stood by the coffin and testified as to how close their friendship was and all the contributions she done give the community. Two of their children had already started families of their own and claimed she'd been a great mama for them and would be so missed by her grandchildren. When all had said their piece, it was old We'yum's turn to express himself."

"You should know, son," Dad says, "no one should say anything bad about the dead. They may come back and haunt you."

Jove goes on. "We'yum began by prayin' and jumpin' around the coffin. He be prayin' so hard an' jumpin' around so much to prove his love, he closed his eyes and fell to the ground, so that everybody believed his sincerity. He rolled around, kickin' his feet this way and that, and accidentally nudged the table holdin' his beloved wife's coffin.

"Rigor mortis caused her body to sit up with her arms reachin' out and her eyes wide open." Jove stretches out his bony arms, and wobbles side to side, imitating how she must have looked. He stares deep into my eyes and blinks. "Now picture this. That there room was noisy and loud with the 'uhums,' the 'amens,' and the 'yassums,' as We'yum prayed hard and loud to the Almighty God, just askin' Him for one more chance to hug and kiss his Tammie Mae and tell her how much he loved her. Then the room went quiet. The only voice y'all could hear was his.

"Standin' back up, openin' his eyes, and lookin' at the crowd first, We'yum looked baffled. He ain't turned round to see the coffin. Then he does, an' he sees her sittin' up with her eyes bulging and arms stretched out toward him. In the corner, leanin' on the chu'ch organ, was a long, thick stick. That We'yum, he picked up that stick and held it high, way over his head.

"'If you ain't dead yet,' he said, 'I'm going to swing this here pole and make sure you is dead.'

"Everybody heard him. Yes sir, everybody heard him."

CAN'T SLEEP

25.

Two weeks have gone by since our arrival. It's our second Saturday evening in Winona. Tomorrow, we're going to church. Instead of climbing into bed now, I wish the night was over and we were heading our way there. Mom and Aunt Myra, wearing their pink-and-white nightgowns, stop to look in on us. Dad sits on the edge of our bed dressed in his navy-blue pajamas with narrow, white, crisscrossed lines.

"Good night, little men," Aunt Myra says, bending over Charles to kiss his forehead.

"Good night, Aunt Myra," we say in unison, harmonizing in various keys, almost competing.

"Sleep tight, boys," Mom says.

"Good night, Mommy." We take every chance to show her our deep love.

Charles ups the ante, saying in his most endearing voice, "I love you, Mommy. I love you, Aunt Myra."

James chimes in. "I love you, too."

Squabbling to show affection, we respond, "Good night, Mommy."

In Charles's most charming tone, he ups the ante. "I love you, Mommy. I love you, Aunt Myra."

James takes the lead of the free-for-all of *I-love-yous* that ensues from each of us in our sweetest, loudest, and funniest way.

"Okay, boys," Dad says, breaking up the ruckus. "It's time to go to sleep. We have a big day tomorrow." His deep, melodious voice is so hypnotic, I fall asleep before the lights are off.

Sleep is peaceful and easy at first, but eventually, I awake to voices coming through the walls. My eyes open to see flickering lights dancing on the closed window shades. My brothers breathe quietly.

I slide out of bed and creep to the living room on my hands and knees. Dad's warnings not to get up play across my mind. I stay out of sight behind the slightly open front door. Several old cars and pickup trucks line the road, motors running, and headlights aimed at the house. Voices from a milling crowd rumble above the din, but I can't make out what they're saying.

The yard is full of people pacing back and forth. Two men sit on the hood of our Packard, and four sit on its roof. I recognize the blonde girl and two younger boys from outside church last Sunday. They're bouncing on the low-hanging limb of the catalpa tree.

Most of the people are dressed in ordinary farm clothes, but nine wear white sheets; two of them are bare-headed, while the others have pointed hoods. Many of the trespassers carry flaming torches. The orange glow of the torchlights rage across their faces. The acrid burning smell of coal-tar pitch assaults my nostrils.

The flickering torchlights illuminate Mom and Aunt Myra. They're at the far end of the porch, holding onto each other. A short, heavyset man wearing a pointed hat stands near the open front gate. He's dressed in a white robe and clutches a Bible in his right hand. He towers over someone kneeling in front of him.

Nothing makes sense. Through my sleep-clogged drowsiness, I strain to hear what the fat man says.

"Y'all know who we is, Niggah," he bellows. He hooks his thumb in the sash and lifts the Bible to the night sky. "Y'all know'd us since you was born, and we done know'd y'all. Y'all know what we expect from Niggahs around here?"

"Yassuh," mumbles the kneeling man, his head bowed.

I hear the words but can barely understand what he's saying.

The boisterous crowd shouts as they listen to the white-robed preacher talking down to the man. "Niggah, we know'd y'all as a young Niggah, helpin' Myra Moore pick cotton for Mister Johnson."

"Yassuh."

"Cain't imagine what y'all did after y'all done left Winona, but y'all ain't goin' to bring no cotton-pickin' ideas here, confusin' folks. We done seen y'all's children in town. Keep them out of the white folks' yards. Teach them their place when they see the white man. Or I will."

"Yassuh," is the only answer the man gives. He shifts, leaning more on one knee, then back to the other. I can hardly make out what he's saying.

Then the torchlight reveals the pattern on the man's pants. I recognize the crisscross lines. I know his voice.

Dad!

In a gruff voice, the preacher continues with his scathing words while thumping his well-worn Bible. The mob roars its approval of everything he says.

"Yassuh, Preacher Brownfield," Dad says.

Dad, you know that man's name! Who are all these people standing around, gawking? Why are they here? Stand up, Dad. Tell them who you are!

My face feels hot, and my heart pounds in my ears as I watch him on his knees, allowing this man to talk to him as if he's dirt. Dad uses that uneducated speech. At home, no one dares speak to him that way.

"Boy, that Catholic chu'ch ain't y'alls chu'ch." The man paces back and forth in front of Dad.

He looks away toward the crowd and again replies to the preacher, "Yassuh."

"That there chu'ch is for them white Catholic folks. Niggah, ain't y'all know that?"

"I knows that, Mister Brownfield. I knows that."

"We ain't gots no Niggah Catholics in this town. Catholics ain't Christians like us. Ain't you a Christian, George?"

I don't like what this man's saying about my church.

When Dad answers, "Yassuh," my anger increases.

This isn't how he speaks. This isn't who he is. But at the moment, he sounds like them. I want to run out there and tell him what he should say to these people.

But I don't.

"Y'all done grew up here, but y'all's family's a bunch of California foreigners comin' here just a thinkin' they'll change the way we live. Niggahs round here is *happy Niggahs*. They like the way we do things. Y'all need to take y'all's Niggah family back to California."

The restless crowd yells, "Tell it, Brownfield!" and, "String 'im up, Preacher!"

"Niggah!"

"Yassuh."

"Y'all see that there old catalpa tree yonder?" The big bully points to the tree, where the girl and two boys sit. "If y'all take the family to that there chu'ch again, we goin' to tie a noose around y'all's neck and leave y'all's Niggah hide swingin' back and forth right there. Y'all hear?"

I clench my fists and almost scream. *Say something, Dad! Stand up! Show these people you're better than them. I don't want to be in Winona. I wish you'd never brought us here.*

"Y'all one lucky Niggah this time, George. Do as I say, 'cause if you don't, y'all's ass is mine."

"Yassuh."

"Stand up, Niggah."

Dad struggles to his feet, his shoulders drooping and his eyes downcast. The preacher turns to the unruly crowd and lifts the Bible above his head. Many in the horde press around the preacher, while a woman, clad in a white robe places a torch in the man's other hand. He waves it in a wide arc above his head, showing its flame to the people in the back. "The Lord has given me a vision. The power above and in me will keep them Catholics away from our Niggahs. This Niggah knows his place ain't with them folks. We got a cross to burn at a chu'ch," and then he strides away.

The youths slide off our car. One of them bangs the hood with a crowbar. Another spits at Dad. I hear low muttering as the crowd disperses. Someone throws his torch on the ground and walks away. Those not walking climb into their old jalopies and drive off.

Mom lets go of Aunt Myra and hurries to Dad. A woman trips her, causing Mom to fall flat on her belly. No one helps her. She lies there for a while, winded. She struggles to her feet and wraps her arms around him. Together they watch the searing lights recede with the people, then they turn to the house and slowly push through the gate.

Aunt Myra picks the lit torch off the ground and faces her house. She looks to the ground, puts her hand to her forehead, and walks toward the back yard, with the torch's flame reflecting off the store and house, lighting her way.

I crawl back to the bedroom and slip under the bed covers, hoping not to awake my brothers. My eyes are closed tight, holding back my tears. I listen for Mom and Dad to come inside the house.

PRETENSE
26.

Sunday's sun is finally above the eastern horizon. I get dressed for church and sit on Aunt Myra's hope chest by the window. My brothers awaken, and James helps Charles find his clothes. Once dressed, they all hurry out of the room. I sit on the edge of the bed, looking at my hands, not thinking, not moving, not anything.

Michael pokes his head in the door. "Gaylloyd, we're ready to go."

I take my time to prepare myself.

Mom and Dad look harried, Aunt Myra is still in her room, and my siblings are outside. As I join them, I wipe my hand on the car hood to feel the dent.

My brothers are jubilant, piling in on top of each other and competing for their favorite seats. I'm the last to get to the car, so I find a place in the back, sit Mark on my lap, and wrap my arms around him.

The car seems to groan when Dad turns on the ignition and eases onto the dry gravel road. "We're going to church in Greenwood this morning." His voice is slow and heavy. "It's going to take us a while to get there. It's about twenty-eight miles away."

Neither of my parents say anything about last night.

Dad continues talking about Greenwood. I lose interest; my stomach's in knots. I wonder if he can see my pain. When we finally arrive in the new town, Dad finds the church and pulls into the lot. Because it's crowded, he drives to the back before finding a parking place. "We're in time for the ten o'clock Mass," he says.

Dad carries Mark. I wait in the car for a few minutes then join my family. I really want to ask Dad and Mom about last night, but I'm afraid to.

Dad leads the family along a walkway to the church. Climbing the steps, Mom winces, grabs a banister, and touches her stomach. Dad holds her arm and helps her up the steps. The red-brick church's bell tower chimes the call for Mass. Colorful flowerbeds and shrubs edge the sidewalk. Across the street, huge, black, wrought-iron letters hang above a playground: *Immaculate Heart of Mary Community School.*

Just like in San Diego, negroes and white parishioners mingle. Several people say, "Welcome."

A white woman who stands at the door and smiles warmly says to Mom, "You have some handsome boys."

After my family finds a pew near the front, I enter and wait in the back. High on the wall are paintings of the Stations of the Cross, beginning with Jesus's sentence to death, and going through the events that led to His being crucified on the cross. I bow my head toward the painting of Him nailed on the crucifix.

I go to the front and sit next to Mom. She looks at me in her gentle way, caressing my knee. Mass slips through time and ends an hour later. Afterward, my parents take us for a walk on the school grounds. Inside the classroom windows are desks, assignments tacked to the bulletin boards, and a chalkboard with the alphabet in colorful lettering above it.

"Just like our school," Michael says.

"Classrooms are classrooms," I mutter.

On the road back to Winona, I barely see the aspen trees and open fields. I don't listen as my brothers prattle on and on. I just want to leave this place.

"I liked the girl in the square-dancing dress," James says to Phillip.

"She said she goes to school there," Phillip replies.

"Mom," Michael says, "I like it here. If we move to Mississippi, I want to live in Greenwood."

"Not me," James says. "I like our school at home."

I look at him and say nothing, just turn back to watch the landscape pass.

Watching the shimmering heat rise in waves above the road is the only memorable event on our drive back to Aunt Myra's. My brothers chatter while my parents and I remain silent.

Along the way, there are no restrooms. Dad pulls to the side of the road to let us relieve ourselves in the tall grass. Other than the sound of an occasional passing car, it is peaceful and quiet. In the sunny midmorning stillness, among dense trees, I see daisies, tall waving grasses, and small ripening melons on meandering vines that grow alongside the asphalt road.

My mind stays focused on what I witnessed last night. "This place is evil," I whisper to myself.

THE HOSPITAL
27.

The changing visions, clashing colors, and burning images that swirl through my dreams quickly dissipate when Dad's urgent demands break through.

"Wake up, son." He shakes me. "We're taking your mother to the hospital."

In a drowsy stupor, I stumble from bed without any questions, pull my trousers on over my pajamas, and, following Dad, rush onto the porch without shoes. Aunt Myra stands near the door in her robe, one hand to her mouth, the other on her waist.

Dad opens the front passenger door. Mom is slumped on the seat. I brace her, so she doesn't fall out, and scoot in next to her. She moans, something I've never heard her do before. A green robe drapes her shoulders and hangs over her bloody nightgown.

"Your mother is hemorrhaging," Dad tells me as he starts the car.

I listen to her breathe and try to be as strong as Dad would want me to be. She rests her head on my shoulder, and I hold her hands.

Dad speeds through the neighborhood, our headlights revealing the ground just ahead of us in the dark. The car bounces at every pothole in the dirt road. Mom makes another low, growling sound. I shudder.

Mom's skin is clammy. My pajama top is already damp where

her head lies. I want her to be comfortable. Not knowing what else to do, I stroke her damp hair.

When we arrive in town, Dad stops in front of bright red-and-white lighted sign for *Winona Hospital Emergency*. Insects dart in and out of the lights. "I'll be back with a wheelchair," he says.

We wait in the car, and I watch him enter the clinic. Mom's heavy breathing is all I hear. "We're at the hospital," I say. I stroke her feverish arms and cheeks.

Dad returns, his face full of fury. "We're not staying. We're going to Greenwood." I don't know if he's talking to me, Mom, or himself.

She moans and calls Dad. "George."

"Mother," he answers, "we'll get there quick."

As we speed away, the car throws gravel into the air and on the walkway. The lights shine through our dust. I steady Mom as much as I can, but the rutted streets jostle us back and forth.

The paved highway is much smoother but has no street lights, so Dad flicks on the high beams and dims them each time a car comes toward us. Insects, lit up by the headlights, swarm across the road. Although we were in Greenwood for Mass just this morning, it seems so long ago and far away. I have no sense of when we'll get to the hospital. Dad pulls into a gas station. "I'm stopping here for gas and to get directions."

The attendant fills up the car and talks to him, all the while spitting on the ground and nodding. A sign over the restroom reads, *Whites Only*. I'm glad I don't need to use it.

We park in a lot near the Greenwood Hospital's emergency entrance. Dad opens the door and takes Mom's arm. She leans heavily on him. He wraps his other arm around her waist and guides her to the door.

"I'm going to faint," she mumbles.

"Get a wheelchair!" orders Dad.

I run ahead, but not seeing anyone or any wheelchairs, I rush back. "I didn't see one, Dad!"

"Grab her arm," Dad commands. "We need to get her inside!"

Her wobbly legs barely support her. She leans heavily on both of us. Dad guides us through the hall into the waiting room and finds a gurney against the wall. We help her onto it.

She sits on the edge. "I'll be okay. I'll wait here until someone comes."

"No, Emma. Lie down," he tells her. "I'll find someone to help. Gaylloyd, get your mother's overnight bag. Aunt Myra put it on the back seat."

"Yes, Dad." I dash to the car.

When I get back, I hand it to him. Mom's head is resting on a pillow, and she's covered with a light-gray blanket. She looks at me and squeezes my arm.

"Son, stay here with your mother. I'm going to talk to the attendant."

He's back in a few minutes. "Mother, a nurse will be right over. I'll stay with you until she gets here. Gaylloyd, wait in the lobby." He points to the waiting room. A sign above the entrance reads, *Colored*.

Two couples, one with a small child, are seated near the back. The child coughs and gags. I walk past them to find a seat. They look up and nod.

I mumble, "Morning," but sit away from them and thumb through an old magazine. I walk around to read the wall posters and try to understand what's wrong with Mom. The attendant crosses the lobby to a man with crutches. The people are either in pain or waiting with them. I pick up the magazine I've looked through twice but haven't read.

Dad appears next to me.

"Will Mom die?"

"Your mother is spending the night here. The doctors need to watch her and make sure she'll be all right." His voice is strained, and his eyes are watery. "We'll go back to the house. She needs to rest, and there's nothing more we can do. She's in good hands here. I'll come back tomorrow and get her."

"What's wrong?"

Dad sits next to me and looks at the floor. "Mom had a miscarriage." His eyes rim with moisture. "We lost our baby."

I stand. "I didn't know she was going to have a baby. Can I talk to her before we go?"

"No, she's asleep. She needs to rest. The doctors want to keep an eye on her and make sure she gets proper care."

Driving home, he grips the steering wheel, knuckles stretched tight. Once we park under the catalpa tree outside Aunt Myra's unlit house, we sit and don't say anything. Dappled moonlight skims through the tree's branches, and shadows dance on depressions in the grass. I stare at the tire hanging from a rope.

THE MARE
28.

The noise of my three youngest brothers chasing one another pries my eyes open. Three short hours of sleep is all I get. I stumble from my room and make a beeline to the privy.

Dad's waiting when I come back inside. "Gaylloyd, I'm going back to the hospital. But first, I'll drop you and your brothers off at my Cousin Vera's in Carrollton. You'll stay with her and her family until I get back. We'll leave soon, so please get everyone ready and tell them to straighten up here before we go."

James and Michael are still in bed. I pull the covers off. "We're going to visit Dad's cousin and her family. Make the bed and straighten up the room and get ready to leave."

"I'm telling Mom you're bossy," says James. "Where is she?"

"In the hospital."

He gasps. "What?"

"Dad will tell everyone about it later. Just hurry. We need to vamoose. No breakfast. We'll eat over there."

* * *

Dad's silence since leaving Aunt Myra's is strange. Typically, he gives us the low down about the people we're visiting, usually accompanied by funny stories where they were kids, like possum hunting or finding duck eggs at the bottom of a pond. Suddenly, he says, "Mom's in the hospital."

My brothers talk over one another, asking what's going on, and why she is there. "Quiet, boys. Just listen. She's there because a tiny baby inside her tummy came into the world too soon." His tone is grave.

"How do babies know when they're ready?" Phillip asks.

I put my finger to my mouth to shush my brothers, to no avail.

"Mom had a baby?" Charles asks.

I do my best to answer for Dad. "No, she lost her baby. It's called a miscarriage."

"Where's the baby now?" he persists.

"I think it's in Baby Heaven," I say.

"What's it like there?"

"Well, it's nice and peaceful, full of angels."

"You mean like that picture of angels at home?"

"Yeah, kind of like that."

"Are there angels at Vera's farm?" Charles asks next.

"Don't know, but it'll be nice there. They have cows," I say, pretending I know.

Their discussion becomes a guessing game about what animals we'll find there. My attention veers off. I hope Mom's okay. I'm sure the blood on her lap was from the baby. Those people with torches and the woman shoving her to the ground caused it. My stomach feels queasy.

If James was in the back seat with me, I'd tell him what I saw. He and I usually talk about everything. He's only fourteen months younger than me and we sometimes feel like twins. I wonder if he would have known what to do when that man called Dad a *Niggah*.

While my brothers talk, Dad focuses on getting us where we're going. Finally, we drive past an unpainted gate next to a split-rail fence that encircles a barn and then disappears into a forest at least a mile back. We stop in front of a green ranch house with a wide wrap-around porch.

In a flowered housecoat, a stocky, muscular woman with soft

brown skin hurries down the porch stairs and over to the car before we can open the doors. For a moment, her broad smile and her outstretched arms distract me from thinking about Mom. We're going to have a good time here.

"My goodness sakes, George, it's sure wonderful to see y'all." She hugs Dad then holds him at arm's distance, looking him over. "Ed! Carmen!" she calls. "They's here."

A brawny man and a girl older than me come down the path from the barn. They're dressed in blue-denim overalls with mud on the knees.

"Here's my family," Vera says to Dad. "We've been doin' chores since early mornin', sloppin' pigs, and layin' out feed for the bulls. I don't think they's done with the milkin' yet."

Ed shakes Dad's hand. "I'm glad you're here."

I stand next to Dad, and my brothers fan out to either side of us. "These are my boys," he says.

Vera waves him off. "Hush, George, I 'spec they is. Boys, I'm y'all's daddy's cousin, Vera. This here is my husband, Ed, and my daughter, Carmen. She's seventeen." To Dad, she adds, "She looks to be just a bit older than your boy." She points at me. "What's your name?"

"I'm Gaylloyd." It's easy to like this confident, straightforward woman.

"Well, y'all is in time for breakfast. Ain't you hungry?" she asks.

"Yes, ma'am," I say.

"I'm sorry to hear about Emma," she talks to Dad as we climb the stairs to the house. "I'm happy the boys are staying here for the day. We'll watch them. They'll be good, and there's plenty for them to do. You need to spend time with her."

In the living room, a huge picture window looks out on the forested edge of a fenced meadow, where horses graze nearby. Sunlight beams on a rectangular table covered in a plain white cloth. Orange summer flowers in a blue-and-white vase form the centerpiece. Plates, glasses, cups, and napkins sit at each place setting, along with coffee and milk pitchers and a bowl of pears as ripe and golden-yellow as the ones on that lady's tree in town.

"I fixed y'all breakfast. Please be seated," she says to us. "The flowers come from out back. And there's a vegetable garden on the sunniest side of the house. I'll be right back. Carmen, come with me."

She follows her mother into the kitchen. Ed sits at the head of the table and motions for Dad to sit next to him. We boys sit wherever we want.

"George, ain't seen you in a coon's age. We didn't know y'all were visitin' until you called."

"Yeah, Aunt Myra keeps me busy. I didn't think I'd have time to see you. I'm so glad she suggested my boys could spend the day here, while I go on to Greenwood." He pours coffee for himself, something I've never tasted, but I'd like to try. He always tells me it'll stunt my growth, whatever that means.

Vera and Carmen return from the kitchen. They set the crockery platters within easy reach. They are piled with biscuits, scalloped potatoes, ham, and scrambled eggs. Breakfast smells delicious.

"Dig in," she says.

"Is this what you always eat for breakfast?" Michael asks.

"Sho'nuff, honey child," Vera beams. "After all the work around here in the mornin', we're purt near famished by this time. I sure hope y'all's hungry." She serves Charles and Phillip then passes the dishes around to everyone else.

Dad spoons a few bites on his plate to feed Mark. He's apparently not eating.

"George, your children should spend the night here." She looks at Ed. "We'd sure like to get to know your boys a bit better. Lord, no telling when we'll see them again."

Ed says, "In Greenwood, there's a nice roomin' house for colored folks. Out-of-towners often stay there. You ought to take Emma there and give her a rest from these hard heads." He looks at James and me and winks. "It might be a relief for Myra to not have the boys underfoot for a day."

Dad laughs. "Well, I think the kids will enjoy running around here. They're good boys. I'm sure they'll like it. They have big appetites." Then his usual joyful smile fades. I stop eating. I wonder if he's thinking about Mom.

James, helping himself to another slice of ham, says, "I'm glad we get to spend the night here. The food's good."

Michael looks out the window. "Yeah, this is a big place. What's around here?"

Carmen, sitting across from her mother, says, "I'll show my cousins around."

"They're city boys," Vera says. "Just make sure they stay away from the bulls."

"Let's go look at the animals," I say, anxious to get outside.

"Y'all just hold on now," says Carmen. "I'll take y'all in a minute."

While my brothers and I wait on the porch, the adults come out. Dad says, "Emma and I will be back tomorrow. We'll stay at that rooming house in Greenwood. You're right—it'll be good for her to have another day's rest. Thanks."

"Don't worry, George," says Vera. "Everythin' will be just fine."

"Bye, Dad," I say, leaning on the porch rail. My brothers follow and wave as he drives off.

"Y'all want to see the pigs?" Carmen asks.

"Sure," James says and grabs Charles's hand.

"Okay, let's go."

"Are you in school?" I ask as we walk down the path.

"Yeah. Next year, I graduate from high school. I plan to go to Tuskegee in Alabama. I like to teach about caring for animals. It's called animal husbandry."

Carmen is tall and strong with shining wide-set eyes. She's dressed like her dad in blue overalls, a blue chambray shirt and black rubber boots.

She stops in front of a pen with six stalls. A huge pig wallows in each one. A pink one with giant black splotches trots up to Carmen, squealing.

Michael steps back. "Do they bite?"

Phillip snickers. "No, silly."

"They might," Carmen says. "Especially that young white sow. She just had piglets." The mama pig is all covered with mud and doesn't look very white at the moment. She lies on her side, nursing six piglets. "This is her first litter, and she's ornery," Carmen informs us. "She weighs almost three hundred pounds. I'll show y'all the barn now."

From the pigpen, she takes us into the barn, where four cows nurse young calves.

"We get our milk from cows with newborns. I finished milking them this morning, but we can get more milk from Betsy." She takes her calf into another stall, grabs a bucket, and places it beneath the cow's udder, puts a three-legged stool next to Betsy, and sits. "Watch my hands. Pull and tighten your fingers on her teat," she explains. With each expert pull, the milk hits the empty galvanized bucket. The sound startles me at first.

Betsy swishes her tail, and the other cows chew their feed. Chickens cluck and scratch the ground around us. As the bucket fills, the sound of the milk softens, and a sweet, steamy aroma wafts up.

"It's y'all's turn to milk Betsy. You, then James, and the rest of you if you want." She gestures to her stool. "Okay, Gaylloyd. Sit here. Now, put your fingers just like I done. Then pull and tighten."

I place my fingers at an angle around one of Betsy's teats, pull, and squeeze. No milk. I readjust my hands. Still nothing. "This isn't as easy as it looks."

Carmen grins.

James nudges me off the stool. "Get out of the way and let me try." His attempt produces the same result as mine: no milk.

"Michael?" Carmen asks.

"No. No way," he says, backing up under a shelf of hand tools hanging on a wall near Phillip. "That cow is way too big for me to touch."

"Well, Phillip?"

"No, thanks., I'll let my big brothers do it." He moves closer to Michael.

"Well then, Gaylloyd, stand here."

I move to where I can see better. She shows me again. I try, but still with no luck. I just don't have the hang of it.

"Okay, James," says Carmen.

Laughing, James sits down. He squeezes one of the teats. Milk gushes into the pail. I wince, hearing the sound, proof that he can milk a cow.

I try again until I get tired with no success. "Let's do something else."

Carmen grabs a bridle off a hook. "Y'all want to go horseback ridin'?"

"Sounds more fun than milking cows," I joke.

We head to a corral, where a chubby horse with gray spots on her hind end stands. She lifts her head from munching fodder and looks up at us. Carmen climbs the fence. James and I slip between the railings.

Carmen strokes her forehead. "Millie's an Appaloosa. The Chickasaws bred them for their looks and speed. Appaloosas have scattered spots like Millie's. She's been around the barn a time or two."

She puts the bridle over her head and leads her around the enclosure twice, rubbing her neck and chest. Then she opens the gate, and James and I follow her to the fence near the house, where she wraps the reins around a post. "She's not a young filly. She knows what to do."

Millie stands next to the rail, waiting for us to get on. I kick my shoes off and climb the fence. Then I crawl onto her back. I sit up, feeling comfortable straddling her middle. My bare feet dangle along her sides.

James gets on behind me and grabs my waist. "We're ready to ride."

"All right, boys, when y'all is ready, click twice. Millie will start movin'. Y'all don't need to kick her. I told y'all she knows what to do. Millie'll pace herself to the rhythm of y'all's clicks." She laughs. "She's a musical horse."

"I'm ready," I tell her.

"Okay, then, y'all's on your own."

Despite the instructions, I kick Millie and say, "Giddy-up," like the cowboys do on television. She doesn't move.

James clicks twice, and Millie ambles away from the corral, her clip-clop synchronized with his click-click sounds. "Yippee!" he yells, and we're off into the wild blue yonder, riding at a leisurely pace, which is thrilling for a while.

When I was five, James and I rode a Shetland pony. Mom said twenty-five cents was a lot of money, but we had fun on that two-bit pony ride. The walker led our horse twice around a corral, and then the ride was over.

There's no time limit on Millie. She'll take us anywhere we want to go on the ranch. We head down the trail. *Clip-clop, clip-clop, clip-clop.* I pull the reins toward the other horses near the woods. Turkey buzzards soar halfway to the moon above them, and crows chase the scavenger birds. And Millie clip-clops away from the corral at her preset pace—no faster, no slower.

"This is great," I say, "but it would be more fun if we went faster."

"Yeah," James says.

We both double-click but don't think about our timing. Like a racehorse, Millie jumps and takes off at a sprint.

I lean forward and wrap my arms tight around her neck, but not tight enough to keep me on her back. I feel myself sliding until I'm desperately holding onto her underside with my hands, legs, feet, and everything I have. Fear keeps me attached.

Realizing her hooves are close to my head, I close my eyes and grasp her belly with my teeth, tasting dust and hay. Her hair bristles against my nose. Her skin smells like stale sweat. I don't know where James is.

Millie gallops to the corral and stops in front of Carmen, who is about to burst a gut laughing.

I drop on my back and scramble between the rails.

James shows up. "I fell when Millie took off," he brags, like falling off a horse is a badge of honor. He has dirt all over his head and body, but he doesn't look any worse for wear, certainly not as rattled as I feel.

"Are you hurt?" Carmen asks him.

"Nope." James brushes dust off his clothes.

"I came out here to call y'all in for dinner. I'm glad I did." Carmen jokes, "You sure made a sight of yourselves."

"Dinner?" I ask. "We haven't had lunch yet."

"Lunch?" Carmen asks.

"It's served at noon…"

"In these parts, we eat dinner around this time of day."

"Back home, we have dinner in the evening."

"That's supper."

I lead the way inside feeling good that I didn't fall off Millie.

Vera asks us, "What happened to y'all?"

"You should have seen us, Vera." James blurts, "We galloped Millie all the way back to the barn."

Carmen cocks her head. "Yassums, y'all shoulda seen 'em!"

Vera shakes her head and points down the hall toward the bathroom. "Well, y'all wash up for dinner."

THE BULL
29.

Vera's handmade soap is made with lye, like Aunt Myra's. After washing up, I scramble to the table.

The food Cousin Vera sets out worries me. Not the smell of the roast turkey with rice stuffing. Not the bowl of gravy next to it or the mustard and collard greens with turnips simmering in their juices. Not the black-eyed peas, ready to be spooned from a huge porcelain bowl onto our plates. And definitely not the cornbread and, good heavens, not the sweet-potato pie on the open window ledge, still steaming.

It's the sheer amount of food.

I nudge James. "Don't eat too much. If this is lunch, and remember all the stuff we had for breakfast, can you imagine what dinner is going to be like?"

James looks at all the food. "You're right. Let's not stuff ourselves."

Vera tells us while we eat, "After dinner, y'all older boys are on your own. Gaylloyd, y'all is in charge. As long as y'all stay away from the bulls and the big animals, I figure you can't get into too much trouble around here."

"One more thing," Ed warns. "Watch out for snakes, especially cottonmouths. They're poisonous. I'm not playin', either. One bite, and y'all be dead in a minute." He gets up and heads toward the door.

Carmen stands. "I got to run some errands with Daddy."

Vera points to Phillip and Charles. "And you little boys need a nap right about now. I have a place for y'all to lie down."

Charles says, "I'm not little."

"Your bed is all ready for y'all. Hear me, Charles? I want no fussin' from you. I got some clothes to wash while the men folks are in town."

"We'll wake y'all when we get back," Ed says.

After they drive off, the three of us go outside, leaving the younger boys with Cousin Vera.

"At Aunt Myra's," I say to James, "I feel like we're always being watched, but here we're free to roam. This is heaven!"

Michael says, "Vera told us we can go anywhere we want," and follows me. "Are you ready for whatever we find?"

"What are you looking for?" I ask.

"Let's take a look at those bulls," James suggests.

"No. They're dangerous, Vera told us to stay away from them," Michael says.

"Well, we passed them when we went to the barn," I say. "I saw them watching us when we walked by. Carmen told us the older one fathered all the calves. The younger bull is his son, but they're not going to sell him like they did his siblings."

"Well, we can go to the corral and look at them," James says.

"Yeah, we can do that," says Michael.

When we get to the bull pen, the older male is agitated, but the younger one ignores us. His horns are shorter than his father's, which are immense. Both animals' horns are tipped with steel balls. The old bull glares, blows his nose, and shakes his head, making the steel tips glint in the sun.

"This one is nicer," James says as the young bull walks over to us and stands by the fence.

Michael climbs on the lower rail. "Would you ride that bull?" he asks James.

"Are you kidding? I know how it feels to fall off a horse. It hurts! No way am I getting on that big animal."

"Aw, come on," he dares.

"I'll do it," I say.

"You can't ride that bull," James says.

He and Michael watch me climb on the top rail and sit like I did before I mounted Millie. Michael stands on the second rail.

The young bull has a heavy collar with a big silver bell. Without coaxing, it moves even closer.

I jump on its back, grab the collar, and at the top of my lungs I yell, "Yee-haw! Ride 'em cowboy!"

The bull spins around, rears, and kicks, trying to throw me off. He tosses his head up, down, and side to side. I'm still on his back, screaming and holding on to the collar with both hands, but the strength and power of this enormous animal scares the daylights out of me. My heart beats so hard, it feels like it's trying to escape my chest.

James and Michael yell my name, "Gaylloyd!"

I'm hanging on for dear life, not hollering or laughing anymore. One hand has a death grip on the collar while the other flails the air.

Suddenly, I fly over the bull's head and land in the mud near the fence below my brothers, who look terrified.

While the bull swerves and kicks up his rear hooves, I scramble to my feet, grab the top rail, and leapfrog out. The bull rams the railing with his horns and pounds the ground with his hooves.

"Did you see that?" I shout. "I rode that bull. Did you see me?"

"Gaylloyd, you're bleeding!" Michael screams.

The bull's horn must have gouged my leg when I flew over his head.

I flop on the ground and pull up my bloody pant leg. "Aw, it's nothin'. Did you see me ride that bull?"

"What a stupid stunt to pull!" Vera stomps up the path, seemingly out of nowhere. "Y'all might have been trampled. I don't know what I'm gonna tell your daddy. Go inside the house. I can't be watchin' everythin' y'all do. I have a lot to do before your daddy gets back here tomorrow."

Back in the Big House, which is what the ranch house is called by Carmen, Vera cleans and dresses my scratches. "It wasn't much.

Y'all's lucky it's just a superficial cut."

I ignore what she says. Now I'm more a daredevil than James and don't have to hear his nonstop boasting about jumping off Millie. Unfortunately, my hard-won bragging rights cost us our freedom.

Vera scolds, "You gotta be careful around farm animals. They ain't like the ones on television."

"Television?" I ask. "I haven't seen one since we left home. Do you have a TV?"

"No, but we watch one at our neighbor's house now and then. All we need most of the time is the Good Book."

Her words transport me to the preacher holding his Bible over Dad's head during the previous night's commotion. That man, and Dad not standing up to him led to Mom losing the baby. The Bible couldn't be what Aunt Myra and Vera claim. If it did, Mom wouldn't have been lying and bleeding on the gurney in a hospital.

After dark, everyone settles down in the living room to read. Vera sits in a rocking chair, reading under a freestanding lamp. She stops and tells us, "I embroidered this lampshade," The scene has a farmhouse and barn with trees in the background.

"It's real nice, Vera. I admired it earlier," I tell her.

I'm almost finished with *Through the Looking Glass*, and I'm hungry. No one seems interested in eating dinner. I try to finish another paragraph. "Vera, is it almost time for dinner?" James joins me at my side.

"Dinner?" Her puzzled stare makes me think she doesn't understand. "We already ate dinner, remember? I thought it'd be plenty to hold y'all until mornin'."

"Oh, we didn't eat much at lunch." I glance at James. "We thought we'd save room for tonight's dinner."

"Y'all two seem to be the only ones hungry. "You must be talkin' about supper. We usually have a li'l somethin' in the evenin' before bed. We're not ready to go to bed, but..." Her face softens as she looks at James and me. "I tell you what. Y'all boys put on your nightclothes, and I'll fix y'all a nice turkey sandwich. How does that sound?"

"It sounds great." James and I rush into the bedroom, dress in the pajamas she laid out for us, and sit at the table ready for *supper*.

"Vera, this turkey sandwich is the best," James says with his mouth full.

"I love the cranberry sauce on the bread," I add. "Next time we have dinner at your house, we'll be ready."

* * *

It's dark when I awake. Carmen and her dad are talking, and I hear their footsteps then the front door close. I dress and find them in the barn. Carmen is brushing Millie. Although I try to milk one of the cows, I still don't have the dexterity, so I carry buckets back and forth to the Big House.

Once we finish, we talk about the work and leave the barn to clean up and eat.

"Gaylloyd, don't worry," Ed says to me. "Milking just takes practice."

I open the door to find Mom and Dad seated on the couch. I'm surprised they are already back. I rush in and join my brothers crowded around Mom. I hug and kiss her on both cheeks. Though she looks pale and tired, I say, "Mom you look wonderful."

She bought a peach-color dress, and her hair is braided and wrapped around her crown. Dad holds her hand. Her soulful brown eyes show a hint of sadness.

"How are you?" I ask.

"Better, son," she says. "Vera has been telling us what you boys have been up to. Sounds like you've been busy." She rolls her eyes.

THE WATERMELON DRIVE

30.

Ed, Dad, Carmen, and my brothers pick watermelons. Mom and Vera stroll on the wrap-around porch. I hold Mark's hand and follow. They stop at the railing for a moment to watch everyone in the field checking melons for their ripeness or carrying the market-ready ones to Ed's truck.

Vera cups Mom's hand in hers. "Emma, another night's rest with me lookin' after y'all, and tomorrow y'all will be as good as new," she says. "It'll be a blessin' for us to have y'all one more day. Sho'nuff, Myra won't mind. George'll call her, and she'll understand. She's always in the store when I telephone her." Mom slips her arm into Vera's, patting her arm with her other hand. "I don't want you to misunderstand why I feel we must leave today. I appreciate the invitation."

"Before George went to get you at the hospital, I asked him what he thought about y'all stayin' a spell. He said it's up to you. I'm sure George will be glad to stay if you want to."

"Let's stay one more night," I plead. "Mom, there's lots to do here. I'm not ready to go back to Aunt Myra's."

She turns to me then back toward the field, where Dad and Ed stoop to tap the melons. Michael struggles to carry one to the truck. Carmen stands on the truck bed, loading watermelons as they're brought to her.

"Gaylloyd, I want to talk to Vera in private. Give Mark to me. See what you can do to help your dad."

"Oh, Mom, I don't want to help Dad. I'd rather stay with you."

"Do what I say. I don't want to tell you a second time."

I walk away but take my time leaving the porch. I hop down one step as if both feet are tied together and then do the same thing again on the next step. I slowly make my way to the field, examining the path. I look back to see if Mom is watching.

"Pick up your feet." Mom sounds annoyed. "Hurry up, and help your dad."

I climb over the fence rail and head toward where Dad and Ed are working. As I pass my brothers, Phillip, straddling an oblong melon, asks, "Do you know how to tell when one of these is ripe?"

I glance at the watermelon, but before I can answer, James says, "Yeah, do ya?" He holds a small, round one with a yellow bottom.

"They look the same to me," I say and walk away.

Dad stands with Ed near his rusty black pickup. "Gaylloyd, help Carmen stack these melons." He pats the truck bed's wooden rails, where several melons are already stacked against the back of the cab. "After it's filled, Ed's taking the load to market."

I shrug. "Sure." I can't look at Dad or listen to him without thinking of him cowering as he knelt on the road a few days ago.

"Your brothers will hand melons to you and Carmen."

My cousin takes one from Phillip and stacks it with the others.

Dad says, "Stand on the far side of the truck bed and place them the way Carmen is doing it."

"George, I'm sure we'll come close to fillin' the truck," Ed says.

I use the rear tire to climb onto the truck bed and stand on one side opposite Carmen. I take a melon from James.

"Gaylloyd, knock on the watermelon with y'all's knuckle like this." Carmen raps one. "Can y'all hear that dull thud? It's ripe." She finds another one, does it again, and looks at me. "That's what it's supposed to sound like."

I tap my middle knuckle on a stacked melon, and it makes the same sound. I try two more. "I can't tell the difference. They all sound alike."

"That's 'cause all these are ripe. If y'all do that to one that ain't ready, y'all won't hear the hollow sound. The one that's green inside don't sound the same as those that are ready for eatin'."

Ed carries a big watermelon to the truck and grunts as he lays it down.

Dad asks, "What year is your truck?"

"I bought it brand new way back in '34. That Ford still runs like a top," he says.

"It looks like you've taken good care of it."

"Yep. One of the things Carmen does before we go in the house for supper is make sure the oil's full and the cabin's clean. Then, we're ready for another work day."

"George, Vera is talkin' to Emma. I hope she wants to stay on for the night. Maybe y'all won't mind comin' with us to deliver these?" Ed looks at what has already been harvested. "Y'all can sit in the cab with me. The kids'll ride in the back."

Dad sets a melon on the tailgate. "No, I'll follow in my own car. Gaylloyd'll ride with me."

"Dad, I'd rather ride in the back of Ed's truck with Carmen."

He ignores my objection and goes back into the field with Ed. I wonder if he knows I don't want to ride with him.

We heap melons for over an hour, until they all but block the rear truck window. There must be around eighty. James follows Dad back to the field to check for more ripe ones, while Ed hands me one more. "We're ready to go, George!" he shouts. "Ride with me to the Big House."

It's almost noon by the time we enter the kitchen. Mom and Vera are at the table with half-filled coffee cups.

"There's the turkey soup Vera heated up, and I made sandwiches," Mom tells us.

Ed kisses his wife on her forehead.

Dad sits down next to Mom. "I'm taking Gaylloyd to the market with me. You'll be all right while we're gone, won't you?"

"I'll be fine. We're staying here one more night, but I think we should return to Myra's in the morning." She takes a sip of her coffee and looks at Dad. "Don't forget to remind your aunt we're heading back to California on Friday."

This is the best news I've heard all week. I keep thinking about the events of last Saturday night. Now that we're leaving, I hope I can forget Winona. I want to go home, where people vote, where I can sit anywhere in the theater, and where what color you are or where you were born doesn't matter.

Before we leave the Big House, Dad says, "Ed, Winona is home for me. Gaylloyd was only a year old when I brought him here to meet Myra. We haven't been back since then. I want to show my boys some more of my home."

We get in the car and soon reach the paved road. During the ride, I survey the flat landscape. Far in the distance, wiry green bushes and small trees border the road. Now, I long for our home, where Torrey pine trees on the high cliffs lean over the San Diego beaches.

"Son, we've all been through a lot this week. I just want to thank you for helping your mom and me."

"*Uh-huh.*" I don't look at him, although I can see his reflection in the window. My mind chews on the memory of the blood on Mom's nightgown and the drive to the hospital, and Dad.

"She could have died." His voice choked.

I turn and look at him. "Why did we have to drive all the way to Greenwood? Couldn't the doctors in Winona help?" I'm surprised at my angry tone, but I don't care.

"Listen son." Dad's eyes focus on Ed's loaded pick-up just ahead, but his voice is stern. "People are different here in Mississippi. Not all hospitals in this state accept colored people. That's one of the reasons we live in San Diego. We don't have to deal with those kinds of things there."

"Well, I want to go home, so I don't have to deal with these kinds of things." I don't look at Dad after that. We follow Ed's truck in silence.

A few quiet minutes pass. Then, out of the blue, he sings, "'Nobody knows the troubles I've seen. Nobody knows…'" and hums the rest of the bars. It's a tune I've heard him sing many times.

Ed stops in the back of a building in Winona. No other delivery vehicles are parked here, giving Dad plenty of room to pull up next to the truck. Ed and Carmen climb out of the cab. Dad and I follow them around to the front of the store, where displays of vegetables and fruits are neatly stacked on tables.

Unlike Aunt Myra's store, this one has no dry goods. The scent of newly picked mustard and collard greens fills the air. Several customers mill around, looking at the produce as they chatter among themselves and fill wooden crates with their choices. Women from Aunt Myra's neighborhood follow white women around and fill up boxes with whatever they want to buy. Several people queue at the cash register up front holding items they're purchasing.

A number of dirt-streaked cars are parked on the street in front, including a white Cadillac Eldorado Seville which is parked under a *"Reserved"* sign.

A dark-haired white man, wearing a denim apron around his bulging middle, walks up to Ed and slaps his back. "Hello, boy. Sure is good to see y'all." He smiles at Carmen and she looks away. "I need fifty melons. That's all I can take. What y'all got for me?"

"Fifty?" Ed says. "Sure, Devin. I got that many. This is my Cousin George. He's with me.

Devin stares at Dad, who looks at the floor and says nothing.

"How much y'all payin'?" Ed asks.

I don't like Devin's voice. It sounds like that preacher's condescending, choking tenor I heard last Saturday night. I have an urge to strike him. I step toward Devin but stop when I feel Dad's hand on my shoulder. I stand in front of the man and then back up until I'm next to Dad.

"I give you a half-cent on the pound," he offers.

"I can't do that. That's last year's goin' rate. To make ends meet, I need two."

"How can I see a profit at that price? Tell y'all what, Ed. I'll make it a cent on the pound. That's double my first offer."

"Make it a half more, and I'll leave ten extras at no cost to you."

Devin looks sideways at his customers. "Nigger, that'll sound good if you take one and a quarter and ask for no more than that.

That's my final offer. Take it or leave it."

Ed looks at Carmen, wags his head and answers with one word. "Deal."

When we get back to the truck, Ed tells Dad, "Devin talks like that. When we was kids, his father told him bargaining is good business. I start high 'cause I knows he'll say something lower. He's a good man. We get along."

My jaw tightens. If I was sure the preacher and Devin were the same person, I'd tell him there's no reason for him to disrespect my father. The Bible teaches people to treat one another well, not to threaten them with hanging. He's not a good man.

The four of us unload the melons onto a wagon, and Carmen and Dad push it to the front. Devin comes to the back while we're working and raps one of the watermelons. "Ed, I changed my mind. These are some nice melons. I'll take all y'all got for two, like y'all asked."

"That's kind of you."

Devin regards Dad for a second, taps one of the watermelons, and leaves.

After weighing it, Dad places the last melon on the ground in front of the vegetable stand with the rest and rubs his hands together, cleaning soil from his hands. "Ed, I need to get going, unless you need our help finishing up this order."

"I'd like to pay y'all somethin' for all the help."

"Don't you dare. We appreciate all you've done for us. I'm gonna drive through my old stomping grounds with my son for a bit. Don't worry about us. You'll probably get back home before we do. Tell Emma we'll be fine."

"Okay. See y'all back at the Big House."

"Gaylloyd, we're leaving. Get in the car."

"What? Yes, all right." I have no idea what Dad's plans are.

Dad gets in the car after I do. "What are you daydreaming about? Are you worried about Mom?"

"It's nothing." He doesn't know what I saw last Saturday night, but it's all I can think about now, especially after seeing Devin. I don't want to talk to Dad about him, but I do wonder why Dad is afraid of him. I want to forget about this place.

He starts the engine and eases onto the road. "Sister and I used to come here with Aunt Myra." He laughs. "We'd walk to the cotton fields before the sun was up and work until after sunset. Folks here say it's workin' from 'cain't see to cain't see.'"

"Are we going to the cotton fields now?"

"We'll drive by there. Crops are rotated. Corn may be growing this time, instead of cotton."

I'd forgotten Dad's promise to show me the fields where he worked.

"Dad, when you took Mom to the hospital, you said she had a miscarriage and lost the baby."

"That's right son. Do you know what that means?"

I shake my head no.

He pulls the car over to the side, turns off the motor and faces me. "A mother carries a baby in her tummy for nine months. If the baby is born too early, it can't survive outside her body." He slumps and his voice trembles; he clenches and unclenches his hands. "Your mother was three months pregnant, so the baby didn't have enough time to finish growing before it was born. That is why it died. It's called a miscarriage. She could have died from losing so much blood. We lost our baby and we almost lost Mom." I've never seen my dad so emotional.

After a few silent moments, Dad drives down the road again. At a turnoff, he drives along a dirt track just wide enough for our car. It's rough, and the car bounces through ruts before he makes a left turn and stops. I roll down my window. Dust billows inside.

We get out and look around. Plants covered in fluffy white balls in prickly brown cups line both sides of the road. I pull a soft tuft out of its pod and squeeze. There are hard, brown seeds bundled inside. Dad leans against the car, watching.

The fields stretch to the horizon in all directions, full of plants some higher than my head. I snap a cotton-covered branch to examine in the car. Purple Martins sing peacefully somewhere in the distance.

I want to tell my dad what I saw Saturday, but I'm sure that would anger him, because I got out of bed after he told me not to. He might also feel bad if he knows I saw him cowering in the dirt in front of that preacher.

It's too quiet out here. I wish I could sprout wings and fly home right now.

THE MISSISSIPPI DRIVING LESSON
31.

After driving alongside the fields for a while, Dad pulls over and stops. "Gaylloyd, if you can help with the driving, we'll get back home to San Diego faster. Now that we're on a road and not in a parking lot, you can get a better feel for being behind the wheel. Let's review what I taught you before, and then I'll have you practice. How's that sound?"

"Dad, wow! That sounds good." I scoot over to the driver's seat. His confidence in me learning to drive instantly changes how I feel. He walks around the car and gets in.

"The points I want you to remember are...." He reminds me about the dashboard panel, the brakes, the accelerator, and all the things he showed me in St. Louis. "Don't forget to use your mirrors."

I'm nervous.

"Well, do you have any questions?" His serious expression doesn't dampen my excitement.

"No."

He nods then looks straight ahead. "Let's go."

I'm not sure if he's joking or being sarcastic. "Okay. Right now?"

"Yes, now! It's what we're here for."

I put my foot on the brake pedal, stick the key in the ignition, turn it, and release the hand brake. The engine's soft purr vibrates my seat.

I look to see if any cars are headed my way, then guide the Packard off the gravel onto the main road. "Where're we going?"

"The speed limit around here is about fifty miles an hour. Head to Aunt Myra's, and then we'll turn around for one more night at Vera's."

I know better than to rock the steering wheel. This lesson is easy. The road is straight, so I can follow it simply enough. We are only a half mile from Aunt Myra's tree-lined community when we turn back toward Vera's.

"You're doing well," he says. "I'm proud of you."

I glance at him. He's always been my hero. I want to please him, but I'm confused and disappointed. Why does he treat the white people here in Mississippi differently from his friends in San Diego?

Before long, we pass Devin's vegetable store. Ed's truck is gone, but Devin's Cadillac Seville is still parked in the same place.

Dad glances at the store as we pass. "Ed and Carmen must be back home by now."

"Do you know Devin?"

Dad furrows his brow and looks hard at me. "Why do you ask?"

"Just curious."

He doesn't answer.

There are things about his life that Dad doesn't talk about. Same with me, like what I know about last Saturday night. Frustration and anger are easier to feel than to admit, especially to him. I put this thought aside and focus on my drive to Vera's house.

With nothing to do but watch the road, I practice the skills I've learned. I check the rearview mirror. A white car, heading in the same direction we're traveling, is far behind us. It's the only other car on the street besides us.

"Dad, I think I see Devin's car." I look at the mirror again to make sure.

He turns around in his seat. "Yes, it does look like his Cadillac."

I increase my speed.

"You don't need to go any faster. Let him pass."

"But—"

"But what?"

"Aren't you afraid of him?" I wait for an answer.

"Why would I be afraid?"

"He's getting closer, Dad. Do you think he knows our car?"

"He might. If he catches up with us, just let him go by." He glances at the dashboard. "Don't forget what you're doing. Watch the road, stay under the speed limit, and pay attention to what's ahead of you. Do you remember what the speed limit is?"

"Yeah, it's about fifty." I check the speedometer.

"That's right, son. You catch on quick."

Farther ahead is Ed's old truck, bouncing around on its suspension. It's quite a distance away, but I can tell I'm getting closer.

"What will Carmen say if she sees me driving?"

"She won't know we're behind her if you don't get close to the truck. Besides, Devin may be in a hurry. It's difficult to pass two cars at one time. Give him room to come back in this lane after he goes by us. He'll need time to check that no cars are coming this way in the other lane before going around Ed's truck."

"The Cadillac is going to pass us." I release the pressure on the accelerator.

It is Devin. There are others with him in the car—a woman, a girl, and two boys. I recognize the girl. I saw her last Saturday night. She was one of the kids sitting in the catalpa tree. I think the boys were also there. They must be her brothers.

I glance at Dad. He's eyeing Devin.

As they pass, Devin slows and looks at me. His wife is saying something to him and shaking her head. His children gaze at us. I wonder if they recognize us from church. They were also standing in the crowd at the end of Mass during our first week in Winona.

"Dad, why are his kids staring at us?"

"Keep your eyes on the road."

Devin accelerates, pulls ahead, and then eases in front of us. A while later, he approaches the truck and passes it. We're still far behind Ed, and I watch the Cadillac until it's just a white dot in the distance.

"Pull over. You did great. I'm going to talk to Mom about you helping me drive home. Don't say anything to your brothers, though, until I do."

Relieved that Devin is gone, I bring the car to a stop. Ed and Carmen probably haven't noticed us and continue on.

AUNT MYRA'S CHURCH
32.

Going to a non-Catholic church will feel strange. We're about to head for Aunt Myra's church in Kilmichael, about eleven miles southeast of Winona. Afterward, we'll leave for San Diego. We're dressed in what we normally wear to Mass, our Sunday-go-to-meetin' clothes.

By midmorning on our last day in Winona, our car is almost packed, and everyone is in a hurry to leave. Aunt Myra and the people we've met since we arrived arranged this special church service to wish us farewell before we start back to California.

Phillip and Michael rush to finish packing the things Aunt Myra and Vera have given them, including water and snacks.

Phillip says, "I don't feel good about leaving Aunt Myra. I wish she could come."

"Me, too," says Michael.

Mom opens the porch door so we can carry our luggage out to the car. "Your aunt has done a lot to make us feel welcome."

I follow Phillip and Michael but stop in front of Mom. "When we get to Aunt Myra's church, I'm going to stay in the car. I don't see why I have to go. At school, the priest says Catholics can go only to Catholic churches."

Dad's turns to me as he places the lid on the tape recorder. "What are you talking about? Of course, you're going inside. The least you can do is to show her some respect. She invited us to give her blessings. You don't know when you'll see her again."

I turn my back to Mom, drop my suitcase, and ball my hands into fists. "I'm not going. It's sacrilegious and a mortal sin. One of the worst things I could ever do."

"You're going." Dad rises from his crouched position. "I don't want to hear another word about it! You're going!"

His anger intimidates me. My body shakes, but I face him and don't back down. What would Jesus's apostles say to change Dad's mind? I shout at him, "You're not a real Catholic!"

Mom takes me by the shoulders and turns me around. I look directly into her eyes and wait for her to say something to Dad in my defense. But instead, she says, "This will be your first time hearing Aunt Myra preach. Maybe you'll learn something."

"I'll learn something all right. Her church is some kind of African voodoo and Indian superstition. It's not Catholic. What can I learn from that?" I pull away from her. "Why aren't any of our relatives in Winona Catholic?" I look around at Michael and Phillip staring at me. They've never heard me talk to our folks like this.

"Mom, you understand, don't you?" I want her to tell me yes. I need her to.

"Gaylloyd, I'm glad you're loyal to our faith, but today, I want you to be accepting of other peoples' beliefs." She leaves me at the door.

Dad snaps. "That's it!" He grabs me and forcibly turns me toward the car. "Get in there, and I don't want to hear another word. Sit in the back seat!" Still upset, he hollers, "James, sit up front. Make sure everyone is in their place. We're leaving now!"

James gets in front, and Dad puts the recorder in the car. I kick at a chicken in my path. It squawks and flies out of the way. I don't want to look at Dad, so the perfect spot for me to sit is behind him.

All is quiet for a moment as I climb in, slam the door, and look around. My brothers move to the far side of the car and talk amongst themselves.

I gaze out the window and close my eyes.

Oh God, I pray for forgiveness. I don't want to go to Aunt Myra's church, but I have to do what Dad says. Please, God. I'm doing my best to honor my father like it says in the Ten Commandments. Amen.

* * *

Dad parks in front of a white-paneled building that looks like the Catholic church in Winona. The pointed steeple has a white cross on top that is similar, but not quite the same. As soon as Dad takes the keys out of the ignition, everyone but me gets out.

"George, how y'all doin'?" asks a woman, as she walks past and toward the entrance.

I don't know who she is or the man accompanying her, but I recognize Hattie and her brother, who follow them. I haven't seen them since we went to the movie. Hattie looks nice in her Sunday clothes. She waves and joins Mom and my brothers.

Dad opens my door. "Are you coming?"

"Yes." But before I climb out, I stall and watch more people walk in. They look like churchgoers anywhere. Most of them, I even recognize. They're Aunt Myra's relatives and neighbors. I wonder how many relatives I have in Winona. They're her kin, which means they're my kin, too.

They greet one another with great enthusiasm, as if they haven't seen one another in years. Aunt Myra, wearing a white, satin robe over her dress and the hat Mom brought for her from home, stands at the door, talking to parishioners as they walk in.

Everyone is dressed in their finest. Vera looks regal in her fancy bonnet with peacock and pheasant feathers. Many women wear brimmed hats that encircle their heads like halos. Carmen, in a colorful summer dress, looks much more grown-up than yesterday.

Dad is behind me when I catch up with Mom. She waits for us on the wooden walkway that leads to the door. Her hat, the one she made for our trip, is also trimmed with feathers that bow every time she dips her head to greet people and dance while she thanks them for coming to see us off. I wish I could be more gracious like her.

Men and women walk arm in arm. The older men wear black or gray suits. One younger man sports a green, double-breasted sportscoat. Another's jacket has rust-colored, pointed lapels. They draw a lot of attention from the young women, even though their fathers are close by. My suit is navy, like Dad's and my brothers'. Vera is involved in a conversation with Aunt Myra, shaking and nodding their heads *no, yes, no,* and *yes* again. I'm not close enough to hear what they're saying.

I watch my family go inside the church and decide Mom might be right. I'll listen to Aunt Myra. Maybe she'll say something important. I slip inside the front door and stand in the back. The furniture is similar to every Catholic church I've attended, with about a dozen polished pews facing the pulpit, each with prayer books and hymnals nestled in wooden pockets. There are no kneelers or statues in this church. A painted white cross hangs high on the wall above the altar. I wonder how these people pray and whether or not God can hear their pagan words.

Behind the pulpit is an organ with a few more pews on either side, facing the audience. Back home, parishioners sit in front of the altar and the choir sings upstairs in the balcony at the back of the church.

A joyful hymn begins, and a procession of parishioners forms in the back, with Aunt Myra following everyone into the sanctuary. They sing as they go up the aisle and find a place to sit. Aunt Myra takes her place at the podium.

I haven't yet decided if I should stay. I'm not sure if I'm committing a sin, even though I've prayed for forgiveness. Just in case, I stand behind the last pew, so I can slip out easily. An usher closes the door behind me and offers me a seat in the back. I shake my head no. Dad leaves his seat up front next to Mom and comes toward me. Aunt Myra watches as he stuffs a hymnal into my hands. When he returns to his seat, the service begins.

Aunt Myra raises her arms. Her robe billows like angel's wings, and the people burst into song.

I refuse to sing. Does Mom notice the differences between this church and ours? Is she as uncomfortable as I am? Dad seems at home, but these are his heathen roots. His baritone voice belts out over everyone else's singing "Rock of Ages." My brothers seem to be doing their best to follow along, but it's a hymn we don't sing in our church. After the song, no one sits.

Aunt Myra prays aloud and quotes from the Bible. The congregation echoes each of her remarks with a cascade of "All rights," "*Mm-hmms*," "Amen, Lord," "Yes, that's right," and "Tell it, preacher."

Preacher? Preacher Myra? I'd never thought of her as a preacher until now.

Many of the parishioners hold their arms high above their head like Aunt Myra and sway back and forth, staring at the ceiling.

One woman chants louder than the rest in an odd-sounding foreign tongue. It seems to go on forever.

When the chanting woman quiets down, Aunt Myra begins her sermon. She talks about my family, congratulates my parents for coming to Winona, and speaks about the importance of our visit to her. She describes the talent show and what a hit was James' "Ave Maria" performance. After a while, my thoughts drift.

Suddenly, everyone laughs, and I jump. I have no idea what's so funny. I'm startled again when everyone begins singing. Once they finish, they sit, and Aunt Myra preaches about the Holy Ghost visiting the apostles. That same woman begins chanting again and sways into the two on either side of her. Everyone joins her swaying. Aunt Myra stops what she's saying. The woman shouts several times, "Amen, sister!" and shakes.

The woman quiets down. The whole church is silent, but even this lack of sound disturbs me. I don't know what to expect. What she says makes no sense; it's gibberish. No one stops her, but they shout, "Alleluia," and "Amen, sister!", egging her on.

She leaves her pew, dancing in the aisle, twisting and swaying as she moves. Then, she glances at the ceiling then the floor and comes toward the back. Suddenly, she stops, and although she's still a ways off, my heart picks up speed. I back up against the door.

She inches closer, raises her open hands up to the ceiling, and says, *"Haka suja genti flanda allemande."* Her eyes roll back. Maybe she's in a trance. I imagine she's calling me. My heart races faster with each step she takes in my direction. I lock my sweaty fingers around the door handle.

Everyone shouts, "Alleluia!" I shove the door open and stumble backward into the sunshine. The last words I hear are, "Come to Jesus!"

I can't get inside the car fast enough. I lock the door, hide below the window, and hyperventilate. I slowly peek over the top of the door frame. She didn't follow.

I'm calm enough to consider returning and climb out. Entering the church, I feel safe near the door. Perhaps Mom and Dad didn't see me leave.

Once the service ends, everyone stands, sings the benediction, and flood like a tidal wave down the aisle and out the door. I step out ahead of the crowd and stand near the front railing. Many of the people know us, at least from the talent show. They fuss over me, asking why I wasn't in the show, and treat my brothers like Hollywood celebrities. I'm grateful no one says anything about me leaving the service early.

With his arm around Mom's shoulders, Dad talks to everyone who comes up to wish him farewell. He seems in no hurry to head home.

"I'm happy to have seen my kinfolk and friends while I was here," he says to Jove, whose Abraham Lincoln smile stretches the freckles on his face.

James leans against the wall and talks to a girl I haven't met. She whispers in his ear, and he laughs, scribbles something in a notebook she gives him, and laughs again when he hands it back to her.

Vera finds her way to me. "I hope y'all visit us again," she says. "We appreciate y'all's help. I'm sure Ed and Carmen would like it if y'all wants to work here next summer. We'll pay ya, of course."

I kiss her on the cheek.

She pulls me into her ample bosom and wraps her arms around me. "Y'all's a fine young man."

While she's talking to me, James joins Carmen and her friends. He shakes Carmen's hand as if he's trying to pump it out of her armpit. "Cuz, I'm really glad we met," he gushes.

Aunt Myra hugs Dad. "Y'all is an example of what you can do with your life, if y'all sets your mind to it." She kisses him on his forehead, tears filling her eyes. Then she turns to me. "Y'all's daddy wants his kids to know and appreciate y'alls' roots. Remember everything he done told y'all. Hear me, boy?" She tugs my ear. Then, taking Mark from Mom's arms, she baby-talks to him. She wipes her eyes with a lacy handkerchief. "Come back soon, y'all."

The entire congregation follows us to our car and crowds around, wishing us a safe journey. Hattie and her mother pull Mom aside, with Charles holding her hand. Mom talks with them while the rest of us wait in the car. All three of them glance over at me as they're talking.

They escort Mom to the car. "Thank you," she says. "I'll talk to him after we're on the road."

Charles gets in the car before Mom.

I ask,

"What were they talking about?"

He shrugs. "I don't know."

HEADING OUT OF SIGHT

33.

Dad and Mom are settled in the front ready to leave. I'm silent in my place in the back seat behind Dad. My brothers climb all over one another fighting turf wars. "Simmer down!" Dad commands.

Aunt Myra stands with her head high, leaning over the church railing, and smiles as she watches us pull away. The entire congregation waves. The farther away we get, the smaller they appear, until finally, as the road bends, they disappear from view.

Dad says, "I'm proud of Aunt Myra."

Mom agrees. "She's accomplished so much. I don't know where she gets all her energy."

Mom changes her tone. "Gaylloyd, Hattie's mother says you took pears without getting permission."

I glance at James. "I wasn't the only one."

"You're the oldest. I expect you to set a good example. That's stealing."

I roll my eyes. "The tree was loaded. Those branches were bent to the ground."

"I know the whole story." She glares at me. "What's gotten into you?"

"But Mom—"

"Don't *but Mom* me." She glances at my brothers. "I expect you to show respect for other people's property. Don't ever let me hear of anything like this again. Understand me?"

I drop my head and look at my hands. "Yes, Mom."

"James and Michael, are you listening to what I'm saying?"

"Yes, Mom," my brothers say together.

* * *

We pass open fields where flocks of small birds soar overhead above scrubby oaks. Trees cluster near weathered fences that seem to hold them in place. The only sounds on this country road are the steady engine hum dueling with the road noise of our tires.

I'm glad we're on our way. I wonder how Dad feels about leaving here. Most white folks in Mississippi are mean. The only thing whites see is skin color. Negroes let themselves be pushed around—like Dad.

A few cattle rest under trees. Others drink from a small pond fed by a stream that meanders into one end of it and trickles out on the other. Dad maintains a speed of fifty-five miles an hour, the same as everyone else on the narrow highway. I struggle to stay awake in the warmth of the day…

I hear Dad say to me, "Use your blinker, son."

I look out the driver's side-view mirror. A white Cadillac approaches. "Dad!" I call out.

He's standing in Aunt Myra's front yard. His skin glows in the flicker of torchlights. He raises his tied hands, and Aunt Myra lays a Bible at his feet.

Voices rumble, getting louder. Groups of negroes carry watermelons to Ed's truck.

A white man, it's Devin I'm sure, dressed in bib overalls, walks up to Dad from behind a cash register at the vegetable counter. "Niggahs ain't allowed in chu'ches around heah," he says.

"Yassuh, I knows dat," Dad says.

There's a huge flag on the store wall with a blue X and white stars in the middle. I'm sure I've seen it before…

I jerk my head off the window. I must have been dreaming, I tell myself. Small wonder nothing makes sense. I listen and look around. My sleeping siblings are slumped all over one another.

"Dad, where are we?"

"We just left Oklahoma City. Glad to see you're back in the world of the living." He shrugs his shoulders and chuckles.

Mom shifts, sits up, yawns, and curves her shoulders forward, stretching her back. "I must have been tired. We've been on the road since morning. George, are you hungry?" She fingers her braids into place.

He glances her way but doesn't answer.

"It's late afternoon." She looks in the back. "The boys are still asleep, but I'm sure they will be hungry. We should stop and get something to eat. A little walk is what you need." She stretches again and twists gently. "Gaylloyd, look in the Travelers' Green Book. Check if it recommends a restaurant around Oklahoma City. After we eat, we'll take a walk."

"Emma, we went through Oklahoma City twenty minutes ago," Dad says. "I don't want to drive back, and I don't know exactly where we are now. We'll try the next place we come to. If we can't eat inside, I'll get take-out."

"Fine," Mom says. "Gaylloyd, please wake your brothers."

I punch James in the shoulder.

"What did you do that for?"

"Mom wants everyone awake," I say.

He hits the others the same way I woke him up.

Phillip whines, "James hit me."

"Cheese and rice." Dad feigns exasperation. "Can't you boys do anything without smacking one another?"

We pass the Blue Barn Eatery. Mom asks, "Do you think that's a good place to stop?"

"We'll just have to find out." Dad pulls off the road and circles back to the restaurant parking lot. Our wheels kick up gravel that pings off the undercarriage. More than two dozen cars are parked in rows near the front.

Mom says, "This place must be popular."

Three light-haired children, younger than Michael, walk out the front door ahead of their parents. Dad parks in the rear and leads us to the back door. We haven't eaten in a restaurant this whole trip.

"Why are we going in this way?" I ask.

"This must be a short cut," Michael says.

Dad escorts us inside. A waitress confronts him at the door. "Yes?" she says as she straightens her apron and pushes her faded red hair off her sweaty freckled forehead.

"I have six hungry boys who want to eat," Dad announces. "Do you have a table?"

She sticks her head into a room just off the back entrance. "Eileen! Will you take care of…" She wrinkles her pug nose. "*These* people?"

We hear a clamor of metal pots and utensils falling. A minute later, a slight negro woman comes out, wiping her hands on her stained apron.

"Y'all please come this way," Eileen mumbles. She picks up a handful of menus and leads us to a small room. Only a few people are there, all negroes. She seats Mom, Dad, Charles, and Mark at a table near the back.

I sit at a table not far from my parents and beckon James, Michael, and Phillip. "Sit next to me, James. I'm so happy we're headed home."

As I open my menu, I watch Dad and Eileen chat. "Boys, I'll order for everyone," he says. "We'll have the meatloaf, mashed potatoes, and green beans. And please bring water for us. Thank you."

On the menu, I read over the dishes Dad didn't choose.

Eileen seems to be the only person working in that room. From the looks of her apron, I would guess she washes dishes when she's not waitressing and busing tables.

Mom comes over to me. "Don't you want to sit next to your dad?"

"No thanks, Mom. I'll stay here." Mark and Charles are seated on either side of my parents. "It looks like there's no room for me."

"I want you to listen to what we're talking about," she tells me. Mom looks disappointed, shakes her head, and sits down. Dad nods at something she says and then glances at me. Eileen carries in two heavy platters and puts one on Dad's table and one on ours. Our conversation soon joins the general hubbub of the room.

"I had a good time," James says. "There's lots to tell my friends." He recalls playing in the cornfield, collecting eggs every morning, and fetching water from Aunt Myra's well.

"She pours kerosene in there to keep mosquitoes out of the water," I remind him.

Michael empties the half-filled gravy boat on everything, even the green beans. "This is good," he says, spearing a piece of meatloaf with his fork.

"It's delicious," I say and take another bite.

Michael and Phillip laugh at Mark when he throws a handful of mashed potato at Mom. Mark giggles and grabs a chunk of the meatloaf. Mom takes his hands and wipes them.

When we finish eating, Eileen counts the money Dad gives her, while he chuckles at Mark's antics. He waves his hand to get our attention. "All right, boys. I see everyone has dined sufficiently."

"Oh, no," I say to James and put my head down on top of my crossed arms. A repeated joke of his I've never understood ends with the words, "...*dined sufficiently.*"

"We're heading out," he says. Then he pulls out Mom's chair and helps her with the baby. "Make your bathroom stop before you get in the car. I don't know how long it'll be before you'll get another chance. We have a long night ahead of us."

As I leave the dining room, I pass Eileen and ask, "Where's the bathroom?"

She points to the door we came in. "Y'all cain't help but see it out back."

Traipsing through the hallway, I say to James, "Look over there!"

James looks in another dining room across from where we ate. "There are curtains on the windows, lamps on the tables, pictures on the wall, and it's packed with white families."

"Around here, white people have separate bathrooms and don't eat with negroes," I explain as we continue out behind the restaurant. "Whites and negroes don't like each other. It's that way everywhere here. I've figured that's the big difference."

"Yeah, like the movie theater in Winona," he says. "I couldn't even go downstairs to buy popcorn."

"They do everything separate, even church. They can't even pray together. I'm not surprised they don't get along."

"The other night, the people with torches in Aunt Myra's yard were white. You saw their faces, didn't you?" James slips ahead of me into the outhouse.

"How do you know that?" I talk to him through the closed door.

"When you crawled out of bed, I wanted to follow, but instead I watched from the window."

"James— You mean, you saw everything? I thought you were asleep."

"Nope. I only pretended. When I saw Mom and Dad coming back to the house, I got in bed. I didn't want Dad to get mad for not doing what he told us. Then you crawled in bed."

"Yeah," I said. "I didn't want him to know I saw him, either."

He slams the door against the wall and bursts out. "I'm going to catch up with Michael." He runs after the rest of my brothers, who are on the way to the car.

Mom is waiting for me in front of the outhouse and walks with me to the car. She stops and says, "I don't know what's gotten into you. Your Dad and I wanted to talk to you in the restaurant, so I asked you to sit with us. It beats the heck out of me why you're avoiding us ever since we left Aunt Myra's."

I'm quiet.

She tightens her lips and looks toward my brothers. "Go ahead and catch up with them," she tells me.

I rush off.

James opens the rear door and gestures for me to sit in the back with him. "I want to ride next to the window. You take the middle."

"*Un-uh*," I say and feel my face flush.

"Gaylloyd, come here." Mom calls before I have a chance to contest James's claim to the window seat. "Your father thinks you can handle the car. With you helping him with the driving, he won't have to stop and rest as often."

I look from her to Dad, their arms entwined. "Mom, you want me to drive?" Maybe this was why she wanted me to eat with them.

"At first, I didn't think it was a good idea," she says. "I don't understand why your attitude has been so poor the last few days." She looks at me as if she wants an answer. "I just don't know…"

"You're almost grown," Dad says. "I told your mother I'm proud of the way you handled the car lessons, how you worked alongside Aunt Myra when she needed your help with the laundry, and how you helped Ed with the farm work. You're confident and mature enough to drive responsibly."

Mom's expression softens. "And you were a big help to your father when I had to go to the hospital. Don't worry, your Dad will be right by your side."

My brothers jump up and down in their seats, chanting in a sing-song voice, "Gaylloyd's going to dri-ive. Gaylloyd's going to dri-ive."

"Dad told me he'd talk to you," I reply, "but I didn't know if you'd agree. Thanks, Mom."

"You'll do just fine." She kisses me on the cheek, hugs Dad, and walks around to the passenger side.

He climbs in on the driver's side and scoots to the center. "Well, son, are you coming?"

I get in and close the door. It feels strange, sitting there with my whole family in the car and me in the driver's seat. I'm so used to just Dad sitting there. My brothers still sing-song their chant as they bounce around in the back seat.

"Daddy, can I drive?" James asks.

"You boys simmer down! Gaylloyd needs to focus." He reviews what he wants me to remember. "When you're ready, start the car."

My gut twists like a ball of rubber bands. I do my best to hide my nervousness, even though I feel ready. I take a deep breath, which gives me some comfort.

"It's okay," Dad says, putting me more at ease.

Before starting the car, I adjust the mirrors and study the dials. I turn the key in the ignition, shift into drive, step on the gas pedal, and ease out to the edge of the parking lot. I stop, look both ways, and ask, "Is it safe to go, Dad?"

"Yes, it's safe. Go ahead."

On the road in the early evening sun, I soon calm down. We pass one Oklahoma cornfield after another, their green stalks turning golden as the light softens. On the western horizon, the sun enflames the wispy cirrus clouds with orange and pink. Flying in flocks, the crows in the distance are probably seeking a roost for the night. Silhouetted against the sunset, bats look like mosquitoes swooping after insects. Oaks, maples, and hawthorns fade to various shades of dusky gray.

Driving feels so different from the lessons in St. Louis and Winona. I realize the enormous responsibility of keeping my family safe. Several cars and huge freight trucks more than twice the length of our car race after me.

"The daylight's fading," Dad tells me. "It's time to turn on your headlights."

I fumble until my fingers find the knob and pull it. On the dark road ahead, white lines glisten. Dad rests his head on Mom's shoulder, and I soon hear his deep, restful breathing.

About twenty minutes go by before I realize everyone is quiet. I glance at Mom. She's looking out the window. The pink gold of her wedding band glows in the soft dashboard light.

James is in the back seat, right behind me. Every once in a while, he tugs on the back of my seat.

"Help me keep a lookout."

"Sure."

I smile at his willingness to help me.

Necklaces of red and white car lights, widely spaced, outline the curving road ahead. All I have to do is follow the red ones in either of the two lanes going west, keeping a safe distance behind the car in front of me. I check my rearview mirror. Oncoming headlights illuminate the inside of the car and shine into my eyes. I remind myself to stay in the right-hand lane, using the white line alongside the road as a guide.

Dad's instructions echo in my brain, and like a mantra, I silently repeat them to myself. I check the mirrors as far behind as I can see, then the sides and look front again. A white car passes me. I watch it speed ahead and overtake other cars.

People dressed in long sheets carrying torches and shouting. They get in the way of seeing Dad's reaction. I crouch on the porch for a better look…

I jump when Dad asks, "Are you tired?"

"No, I'm fine. Daydreaming, I guess."

The speedometer is almost at sixty. I slow down to fifty-five.

Dad nuzzles his cheek on Mom's bare shoulder. I've forgotten James is watching until he whispers, "Dad's gone back to sleep."

I can't talk to James about that night. St. Louis, Memphis, and Winona crowd my thoughts like action movies, while truck engines punctuate the cool night with thundering roars. In the left lane behind me, a menacing hulk barrels down to pass.

James says, "That truck behind us is getting close."

"Yeah." I tighten my hands on the steering wheel.

It approaches, the hum of its heavy engine mesmerizing me. I struggle to stay in control. I can't focus. Instead, I stare at the truck. I can't look away. Its whining vibrato engine and giant size coax me to drift toward it.

Come to me, it calls. *Come to me.*

"I need help," I yell. "Dad! The truck's sucking me into it."

He jumps and looks up then puts his hands on the steering wheel. I tighten my grip and struggle to keep from turning into the truck. Dad fights the pull of my hands and holds the wheel steady. "Slow down, and let it pass."

I let up on the accelerator. A shuddering roar engulfs me, then the truck passes, carrying the sound with it. Dad calmly grips the wheel until everything is smooth again. I pull off the road.

"Better?" he asks.

"Yes, better," I say.

"You did the right thing. I'm proud of you. Tell me what you think happened."

"It felt like it was pulling me toward it!"

"Those big trucks create a vacuum when they pass. That's why it feels like they're sucking you in." He looks at me as if wanting to ask something else but says, "You did well to keep the car going straight. I'm right here next to you. I'm glad you woke me. Wake me again, if I fall asleep."

I don't respond.

"Son, it's all right," he reassures me.

"It doesn't feel all right," I blurt out. "I want you to drive. I don't know what help you'll be if you're asleep!"

"What?"

"You didn't help Mom when she fell. All those people with torches, standing in Aunt Myra's yard looking down on you. I saw you on your *knees*!"

Dad stares at me, and Mom lifts her head from the window. Neither says a word, but Dad's face tightens.

"I thought you'd explain what happened, but you haven't," I tell him.

Mom's fingers squeeze Dad's forearm. "How did you know? When we checked on you, all of you were asleep. You were…" She nods at my drowsy brothers.

"Mom and I need to explain what happened," Dad says, "but this is not the time. We'll talk about it later, after we're all rested. I'll drive."

I look at him. "No."

That word, *No*, surprises me. Strangely, he doesn't insist, like he has a thousand times before, when he wanted me to do something I didn't want to do and keep on driving.

HOME AT LAST
34.

Dad and I develop comfortable driving and sleeping patterns with the car. When one of us gets tired, the other takes over the driving. After traveling a few days, we reach Flagstaff in the late morning and stop for breakfast. The parking lot is crowded with station wagons and regular sedans similar to ours.

A white couple, older than our parents, comes out of the restaurant, beaming with joy. The man's jeans, plaid shirt, and black cowboy boots complement the woman's flared, sunflower-print dress and round straw hat.

"How's the food?" Dad asks.

The man answers with a toothy grin that curls up one side of his mouth. "Wahl, we've been coming here for seven years now, and we've never been disappointed, except once."

"Is that so?"

"I ordered a short stack, but it was so tall, I just couldn't eat 'em all! Those pancakes were good. I shore hated to waste 'em." His head bobs up and down. His wife, smiling and blinking long dark eyelashes in the bright sunlight, leans on his shoulder.

Dad chuckles. "I guess we'll have to watch out for those short stacks."

The couple laughs and walks off hand in hand, swinging their arms to the rhythm of their steps.

As we enter through the front door, other customers nod in a nonchalant way, so different from at the Blue Barn Eatery.

The wallpaper has desert images in dusty shades of red and gold: shepherds guarding their flocks and cowboys branding steers between muted-green saguaro and barrel cacti. This place and these people remind me of Dad's college friend's Italian restaurant we went to before leaving San Diego.

I hear English mingled with Spanish and a third language I don't recognize. James, Michael, and I sit in a booth by the window. Just as I sit down, a roadrunner flees across the rocky landscape, chased by a coyote. Mom sits at a table next to us, near the breakfast counter where a young couple chats.

A tall, brown-skinned, young woman places a tray of glasses and a pitcher of ice water on my folks' table. "My name is Holly, and I'll be your waitress. Breakfast or brunch?" She flashes a warm smile at us and then back to Mom.

"Breakfast, thank you," Mom says.

"I love big families." Holly distributes the water glasses and menus. "Traveling through or will you stay in town for a while?"

"We're on our way back home to San Diego," Mom answers, "and hope to arrive tonight."

"I'm sure you'll be glad when you get there. Do you have any questions about the menu?"

"Not yet."

"I'll give you time to go over everything. I'll be right back."

"I like your necklace. It's turquoise, isn't it?" I ask.

Holly tosses her long, black braids off her shoulders. "We make jewelry right here on the Navajo reservation." She shows us the turquoise and silver ring on her hand. "Stop in the bookstore before you leave," she says, pointing to a glass wrap-around room at the other end of the restaurant. "Get your girlfriend something nice." She grins at me, her braids swinging slightly with the shake of her head. "I bet you have more than one."

I've never had a girlfriend but don't tell her.

Dad tucks a napkin under Charles's chin, while Mom fastens Mark in a highchair. As she pulls the attached tray down over the baby's head, Dad murmurs something that seems to disturb her. She shakes her head and answers quietly. Maybe they're talking about last Saturday night.

I take a sip of water, attempting to cool my anxiety.

After Holly takes our order, I scoot closer to James and whisper, "Why didn't you tell me you were awake? I thought I was the only one who saw those people. And Devin, the man who bought Ed's watermelons, well, I'm sure he is the same man who was standing over Dad that night. I didn't know who I could talk to about it."

When our order comes, Holly serves James and me first.

"*Nizhónígo adíiyįįł*," she says. "It's Navajo, meaning enjoy your meal."

I give my plate a once over, to be sure I have what I ordered. "I'm hungrier than I thought," I tell her.

James pours maple syrup over his hotcakes. She serves Michael and Phillip next.

Michael asks, "What were you guys talking about?"

"Is it about the people who went to the ten o'clock Mass in that tiny church?" Phillip asks.

"This is between James and me," I say, dismissing them.

"They can listen," James says.

I want to know," Phillip scoots closer. "Gaylloyd, you can't whisper anyway."

I tell them how embarrassed I felt, seeing Dad in his pajamas kneeling in front of the fat preacher and what happened at the Winona hospital. "The doctors wouldn't take Mom as a patient. We had to drive all the way to Greenwood. You should have seen the blood on her nightgown. I thought Mom was dying."

* * *

Dad pays the bill. My parents look calmer than earlier. I hope they've decided to explain what happened last Saturday night. Dad holds the door for Mom, and I'm glad to see my parents smiling. Holly calls out, "Come back again."

Instead of going to our car, we walk to a picnic area beside a shallow stream. "Let's sit here." Dad says. "Mom and I have things to say to everyone." We sit around a rustic table beneath a shade umbrella.

"Charles, take Mark's hand and walk around," Mom tells him. "But stay in sight, and don't play in the water."

Dad looks at me with a tense expression. "I'm not sure what you saw or heard last Saturday night."

Mom rests her elbows on the table. "Your father and I have protected you boys from many of the struggles we went through growing up. We want you to have a better life than what we had. We've raised you in a beautiful home, in a good neighborhood, and sent you to private schools."

Dad interjects, "And you've never gone hungry."

"But Dad, you should have told those people who you are."

"Gaylloyd, they know me. I grew up with them. We were childhood playmates. The preacher and I picked cotton together, but we went to separate schools. We compared our school books. His were always newer than mine by several years.

"Are Preacher Brownfield and Devin the same person?" I ask. "They sure look alike."

"Yes, they're the same man," he verifies.

"If your dad hadn't stepped outside to meet that crowd," Mom explains, "they would have come in and taken him. No telling what they would have done to him."

"Those people were angry," Dad says. "I know Preacher Devin Brownfield well. He was trying his best to control the mob. Winona has never had colored Catholics. Growing up, I had only heard stories and jokes about Catholics and thought nothing about them. Not until I met your mom did I learn all that Catholics aren't white."

"What were those people going to do to you, Dad?" James asks.

"Well, son..." He lowers his head. Mom draws closer and puts her arms around him. He releases a big sigh and looks at James. "A long time ago, along with all the colored folks in Winona, I watched a white mob put two men and a woman on a mule and tie ropes around their necks. They threw the ropes over a tree limb and kicked the mule. The spinning rope swung back and forth with the three of them kicking their legs and choking until they died. It was horrible. All the white people in town were there. I remember it as if it were yesterday."

Tears trickle down his cheeks. "I knew them." He wipes his eyes with a handkerchief. "After that, their homes were burned to the ground. The woman had three children. I don't know what happened to those kids. Someone took them in, I'm sure of that."

"That could have happened to you last Saturday." Mom's sad eyes look at Dad.

"Later," Dad says, "Devin and I talked about what happened. It scared us both. When I was older, I went to St. Louis to find my father. Aunt Myra said I could get a high school diploma there, and Devin agreed with her. He told me to get out of Winona. Coloreds can't get a diploma in Mississippi."

"Actually, you were pretty brave to face those people," James says. "If you tried to fight them, would they have killed you?"

I'm suddenly ashamed of how I've acted. Dad must have been scared. He must have known the best thing to do was to stay on his knees, say nothing, and let the preacher talk to him as if he wasn't a man. "Dad," I say, "you *are* brave."

* * *

All the rest of the way, Dad and I take turns driving. When I'm at the wheel, he and Mom rest their eyes, but I know they're paying attention to my driving. Today after lunch, Dad drives for a few hours, and then it's my turn again. Time seems to crawl the longer we're on the road. In the Arizona desert, dime-sized raindrops splatter the windshield. Then, as if falling from buckets, water washes the road and fills all the low spots. As the wipers struggle to clear the windows, I slow down and plow through shallow puddles.

Dad says, "This is a cloud burst. I'm glad you're slowing down. Good thinking." I'm pleased he noticed.

The downpour doesn't last long. Steam rises from the black top, and vertical waves shimmer.

"Now, look over here." Mom points to a desert tortoise trudging along the gravel at the edge of the road.

I pull off and stop the car, so we can watch it amble up the side of the ditch toward a plant loaded with ripe, red cactus pears.

"I like the gray-and-brown patterns on his shell," Phillip says. "He's so well camouflaged, I can only see him when he moves."

"We have that kind of cactus at home," Michael says, watching the turtle chomp into one of the fallen fruits.

I think the turtle's life in the desert is like Dad's struggle in Winona. We are lucky to live in California. It's like a shell that protects us from what he went through. He works hard to give us the things he didn't have as a child.

Back on the road, I come to a huge billboard wedged into a jagged boulder. It reads: *You are Leaving Needles, Arizona*.

"Mom, what does that sign mean?" Phillip asks. "Is Needles the last town in Arizona? Are we going to get home today?"

She raises her eyebrows. "Well—"

I interrupt. "In other words, guys, the next stop is home."

ACKNOWLEDGMENTS

I would like to thank my wife and partner, Kathleen, a kindred sunlit spirit who joined me throughout my emotional travels during this story's writing. She assisted my depictions of the women's viewpoints.

Also, Miguel Scherer, the manuscript's first beta reader; Benj Burke and Beth Hammermeister, who stuck with me through the story's second writing; the Puyallup Starbucks Writers, which later morphed into South Hill Writers; the Renton Writers critique sessions; and the African American Writers Alliance, who introduced live readings to the public.

I want to give specific thanks to others whose distinctive influence moved my story along on its the journey. The following have my emotional appreciation for their help: Georgia McDade Ph.D., Al Rubeck, Judy Kimball, Wally Thurman, Margaret and Don Barrie, Sylva Coppock, Theresa Zimmerman, Ronda Taylor, Cherie Langlois, and Barbara Bina.

Particular acknowledgement and thanks for helping me share the story goes to the Pacific Northwest Writers Association, Washington Lawyers for the Arts, recommended by manager and curator Betsy Fetherston of Columbia City Art Gallery, and to my editors, Laura Watson and Kathryn Galán.

ABOUT THE AUTHOR

Joseph G. Sissón is an educator, philosopher, and natural science writer with membership with the African American Writers Alliance. He hosts three writer's study groups and is a political activist, serving the city he lives in as an Arts Commissioner. He has been a guest speaker for the American Association of University Women, written articles for the University of Washington's *VOICE*, and a newsletter for the horticultural organization, Plant Amnesty. He is a published poet and novelist of short stories. His poetry themes are scientific phenomenon, natural sciences, and personal political opinions.

Down the Road a Piece is his debut novel. The book's genre is autobiographical, historical fiction. This is a coming-of-age story written in the voice of a well-educated privileged child.

Visit Joseph's website at josephgsisson.com

Made in the USA
Monee, IL
01 October 2023

2bbe08d2-8bcd-4fcb-8751-076ad1c433dfR01